Sign up for our newsletter to hear
about new and upcoming releases.

www.ylva-publishing.com

Other books by Cheyenne Blue

Girl Meets Girl Series

Fenced-In-Felix
Not-So-Straight Sue
Never-Tied Nora

Party Wall

Cheyenne Blue

To small Australian towns, red wine, and the yoga poses I'm incapable of holding.

And to D. Always.

Acknowledgments

Thank you to the wonderful people at Ylva Publishing, in particular Gill McKnight, JoSelle, Astrid Ohletz, and on this occasion KD Williamson. These people make me think harder and make me laugh. That alone is worth the pain of a thousand misplaced commas. Thanks also to my friend, Marg, for her careful read. I owe you lunch.

Chapter 1

THE SUN REFLECTED OFF THE window, obscuring the view of the shop inside. Still, Freya was hyperaware of the products on display. She shuffled her feet and coughed, but didn't move towards the door. In the window, she caught the reflection of Carly's easy smile, as if she frequented sex toy stores all the time. Freya moved to one side. Now the sun slanted low, slicing through the glass. A mannequin wearing red-and-black, skimpy, lace underwear caught her attention.

"Tasteless," she muttered.

Carly glanced sideways at her. "I've seen worse in the chain stores in Mackay. I think it's sexy. I'd wear it—if I were ten years younger and ten kilos lighter."

Freya sniffed. "There is so much inherently wrong with that statement. What you wear shouldn't be determined by an outside opinion of what looks good. Your self-worth isn't dependent on another's approval—"

"Okay, okay." Carly's interruption was tempered with a smile. "I didn't mean it quite like that." She pointed to a discreet sign in the corner of the window. "'A woman's pleasure is in her own hands.' Clever."

"Why don't they just show a purple dildo and be done with it." Freya took a tiny step towards the shop next door. Her shop.

Carly shrugged. "No doubt there's some law against it. When did you last see more than lingerie and posters in a sex shop window?"

"I'm not in the habit of looking." Freya's voice was riveted steel. "I'm surprised you are."

"I don't often." Carly grabbed Freya's hand and pulled her back towards the window. "After all, we don't get much chance living here, do we? The last sex shop I saw was in Brisbane when Andy and I went down for the rugby. But that wasn't like this—it appeared to cater mostly to men. This one seems different."

In Freya's jaundiced opinion, that was like calling a spade a manual digging implement. "It's all the same. Catering to the baser instincts of men. Objectifying women. Turning them into sex objects."

Carly turned to face her, and Freya caught the little wrinkle between her eyes. Good. Maybe she was getting through to her friend. This shop was everything she found repellent. Its silver-and-purple paintwork shone garishly in the sun. The wide window showed only the paltry display and a backdrop of black-and-silver cloth blocking the rest of the shop from view. Probably a good thing. Who knew what was behind those folds and artfully arranged drapes? The mannequin was on the left, and the sign Carly had noticed was propped up on the other side. The middle was empty, a blank canvas for... Freya shuddered. What would end up there? She already knew she wouldn't like it.

Her gaze moved right, to her own shop window. A Woman's Spirit. She narrowed her eyes and saliva filled her mouth.

Even the name of the next-door shop, A Woman's Pleasure, was offensive, being so similar to her own. Her shop front was tasteful, painted the silver-green of gum leaves. Nothing stopped a passer-by seeing inside; indeed, the wide window drew the gaze inwards to the welcoming warmth of racks of books and tarot cards, to the stands of bright clothes, the shelves of crystals and pottery.

"It's great that there's a tenant." Carly rested her forehead on the glass and shaded her eyes, trying to peer inside. "It's been a couple of months since Diane moved to the coast. It can't have been good for your business, having a vacant shop next door."

Freya snorted. "Better a vacant space than this. Diane's organic produce shop and mine complemented each other—we got a lot of cross trade. I doubt there'll be any now."

"You might be surprised."

"Unlikely. But it doesn't matter. This shop won't be here long. I'm surprised the council approved the permit." Freya's gaze shifted to the window, where the permit was taped to the glass. "Maybe I should check that they actually did."

Carly huffed a breath. "I think you'll be wasting your time. There's no way the owner could get away with it in a town as small as Grasstree Flat."

Freya shrugged. "Maybe that's what they're relying on."

"Honestly, Freya? Drop it. I'm sure it's fine. Try and give the owner the benefit of the doubt. They're new in town, it's a new business. Surely it's better for you and your shop if they make a success of it." Amused exasperation tinged Carly's voice.

In front of the two women, the black-and-silver backdrop twitched, saving Freya from answering. A hand appeared through the gap and placed down some stands, the sort that might support signage or photographs. The hand was tawny, with short, manicured nails. Two silver rings glinted on the fingers.

Carly nudged Freya. "See? A woman owns it."

"I gathered that already." Freya pointed to the sign that was already nagging in her head, an irritant not to be forgotten, like a mozzie bite on a hot summer day. "I doubt a man would run a store called 'A Woman's Pleasure'."

"Not necessarily."

The hand adjusted the position of the stands. A forearm extended through the curtain, then withdrew.

"I'm going to ring the council."

"And say what?" Carly said in a neutral tone. "That you think the new owner is breaking some law you're not aware of? The window is tasteful, Frey. I quite like it."

"It's only remotely all right now because it's mostly empty. You wait, that mannequin will only be the start." Her fingers twitched with the urge to rant some more, but she controlled it. Deep breaths. A slow inhale, hold that breath, and then let the tension of the moment expel in the whoosh of air through her mouth. She would not let this shop get to her.

On Freya's third exhale, the curtain dividing the window from the rest of the shop was pulled to one side. The owner of the hand came into view. The lighting behind her was dim, only enough to show a smooth-skinned arm, a full shoulder, and the curve of neck and breast. The woman wore a yellow singlet, and a bird's wing of smooth dark hair hung down, obscuring her face. In the dimly lit shop, she was bronze and sunshine, her top standing out brightly against her dark skin, a beacon in the shadows.

The woman placed a handful of lingerie in the window. She piled it in a bunch, with no attempt at display. A froth of lace and bright colours mixed with the darker sheen of satin or silk, something smooth and luxurious. She reached behind her and brought out another sign, which she propped on the stand she'd placed earlier: *Sensuous Reading for Women*.

"Dirty books. Porn." Freya grasped Carly's arm as a prelude to urging her away, into the safety of her shop.

The woman in the window straightened and saw them looking. She smiled hugely, her grin spontaneous and infectious under high cheekbones. Carly grinned in response, and Freya's own lips twitched before she schooled her features back to disapproval. The woman gestured to them with a smile that obviously meant "come inside".

"Let's go and have a look. Meet your new neighbour." Carly took a pace towards the door before Freya could reply.

"Go if you want," she said. "I have a shop to open."

"It's still ten minutes early." Carly glanced back to the window, where the woman watched them. The smile still graced her face, as though she was amused by their dilemma.

"Got things to do." Freya stepped into the porch between the two shop entrances and slid her key into her lock.

The two doorways slanted towards each other: Freya's green door, with the wooden sign stating *Welcome, Friend*. And on the other side, the as-yet featureless black door of A Woman's Pleasure. After a beat, Carly followed her in to her shop. Freya flicked the lights on to full and the familiar space calmed her more than any deep breathing could. Her space. Fashioned in a way to soothe her soul, filled with things that nurtured, that calmed, that strengthened. A Woman's Spirit was an empowering place, one where women could feel secure, could browse and relax in a space where they wouldn't be rushed, or harried, or cajoled to purchase. Freya walked to the back, past the racks of feminist and spiritual literature, past the displays of crystals and stone jewellery. At the back was clothing from hill tribes in Thailand and Nepal, sourced from suppliers who paid the creators—all women—a fair and living wage, and donated a percent of the profits to ecological projects within the villages. The other side of the room had racks of pottery, hill tribe beadwork, and artwork. Himalayan salt lamps glinted in the light from carefully positioned spotlights. Freya moved past the couches set either side of a low coffee table, to the water urn and flicked the switch to heat it.

"Will you be at class later?" She turned to Carly, her words softening as she looked at her friend.

Carly's brown hair hung in disordered array over her face. She grinned in response. "Of course. Wouldn't miss it. I'll see you later. I better get away now. I promised Andy I'd check on whether the tiles he ordered have arrived."

"No worries." Freya stretched up to kiss her on the cheek. "I'm expecting a delivery of tisanes from the new supplier. I'll save you something good."

"Thanks. You're the best." With a squeeze of Freya's hand, Carly was gone, bouncing out into the morning sun. The door, with its Indian chimes, banged behind her.

Freya closed her eyes briefly. Carly was her good friend, her best friend, her long-time friend. But sometimes she was over the top. Too bubbly, too accepting, as she skated and danced her way through life. Freya went into the small kitchenette at the rear of the shop. She really needed a cup of tea, and the urn would take far too long to boil. As the kettle built up its head of steam, thoughts of the woman next door intruded. Sex. Porn. The physical lusts of life.

Everything that she avoided. Everything that she tried to rise above.

The kettle boiled. Freya selected a jasmine green tea, poured water into her mug, and went back to her shop. Time to open up for the day.

Just past five, Freya turned the *Welcome, Friend* sign around and climbed the narrow, rickety stairway to her flat above the shop, stepping past the fourth stair where the dry rot threatened to crumble under her weight. Her cat, Dorcas, greeted her, entwining around her legs in a noisy appeal for love. Freya picked her up and Dorcas snuggled under her chin, purring her appreciation. With the cat balanced on one arm, she made a cup of ginger tea with her free hand.

Freya moved to the front room, where a wide balcony overlooked the street. Grasstree Flat's main street was quiet at this time of day. After most of the shops closed, before the single pub became busy, there were generally just a few people dashing into the convenience store, walking dogs, or ambling home. She sat on the couch overlooking the street, and Dorcas settled on her lap. For a few minutes, she sipped the spicy tea and watched the late afternoon sun slant down the hill to the main part of town. She lifted a hand in acknowledgment to one of her yoga pupils, but didn't say anything. Dorcas's contented rumbling purr and the occasional car driving slowly past were the only sounds.

Until the music started. It wasn't the blast and blare of a car radio turned loud with the windows down, nor was it particularly unpleasant. The salsa beat was catchy and infectious, a happy tumbling of notes. But it was loud enough that it disturbed Freya's space, intruded in her peaceful sanctuary.

And it was coming from the flat next door. The flat above *that* shop. She looked at Dorcas; the tabby didn't seem disturbed; she continued to knead the cloth of Freya's loose pants with her claws.

Someone must now be living there. Or maybe someone was renovating it for another purpose. Diane had had a house in Grasstree Flat where she'd lived with her husband and kids, so although she'd used one room of the flat above for an office, she'd never lived there. The after-hours time had always been Freya's alone.

She sipped her tea and tried to relax into the late afternoon. But it was impossible. The music played on. And then, to make things worse, a loud and off-key voice lifted above the tune, singing in Spanish. Freya waited. Surely, at any moment, a normal person, a *considerate* person would think of their neighbour, and the fact the wall between the flats was only a single skin of wooden panelling. Queensland houses, especially the older ones, didn't have the solidity of build that houses further south in the cooler states had.

The music paused, and Freya exhaled in relief. But then a blast of horns led into the next tune, one that was even louder and faster than the previous piece. Tipping Dorcas from her lap, Freya stood and moved to where her balcony adjoined next door's. A flimsy piece of lattice separated the two spaces. She rested her hands on the railing and leant out so she could see around the lattice to the next balcony.

It was a mess. A confusion of plants in planters and pots were strewn haphazardly across the floor—tomatoes, a jumble of herbs, and some sort of climbing vine. She sniffed. If she looked harder, she'd probably find a couple of dope plants, something that was very definitely not legal. A wicker couch faced the street in front of a low table piled high with boxes, as if the owner had taken the contents and left the empty boxes there to deal with later. No one was in sight, but the music played on, as loud and intrusive as ever.

"Hello," she called. "Can you hear me?"

No one answered.

"Hello." Her voice was nearly a shout, but it still didn't make a dent in the wall of sound. "Can you turn the music down. *Now*."

Still no response. Freya clenched her jaw and stalked back to her own front room. She raised her fist and banged on the wooden wall, once, twice, a third time. The singer next door paused. Freya waited for her to get the hint and turn the music down, but after a few moments, the singing resumed.

The insensitivity of it. Just what she would expect from someone who ran a sex shop. Just what she would expect from someone with no care or concern for people or community. She raised her fist again and banged on the wall in an irregular rhythm, not stopping until first the singing stopped, and then—blessedly—the music was turned down. Freya waited for it to cease completely, and when it didn't, she banged again.

This time, the hint was taken and the noise stopped in mid-note.

Chapter 2

LILY HUMMED UNDER HER BREATH as she put the finishing touches on a display and stood back to assess the impact. By law, customers had to walk around a partition to access the shop, but once inside, they would see that this was very different to the usual sex shop. There were no wall racks holding sealed sex toys, displayed with all the finesse of kitchen utensils. No displays of porno magazines in plastic wrappings, or cardboard boxes containing life-size blow-up dolls, their pink mouths permanently puckered to take a cock. Walking into the average sex shop was like walking into a tacky discount store. But, it seemed, that sterile, functional sort of atmosphere was what the average customer wanted. The average male customer, that is.

Lily's previous store had been exactly like that. She'd managed a busy sex shop in Sydney's Kings Cross. Turnover was brisk, but the average punter stayed only a few minutes. They'd swaggered in, or shuffled furtively, browsed the shelves, swept something up, paid, and then left as fast as they could. She'd dealt with groups of giggling women on hens' nights and the bluster and bravado of blokes let loose from the pub. She had more shoplifters each day than the average supermarket got in a week, and more underage kids trying to sneak in than to any suburban pub on a Friday night.

But A Woman's Pleasure was her store and things were different. The shop was warm and welcoming, almost cosy. Warm lighting, rather than the harsh glare of fluorescent, illuminated sunny tones. The polished floorboards were springy underfoot—a remnant from the previous tenant. Lily had painted the walls a soft yellow, and the side windows had blue blinds. She moved to where four slouchy chairs faced each other across a low table and rearranged the books and leaflets piled on the table—quirky, humorous, educational, or informative brochures, aimed at women across the gender and sexual-identity spectrum. It was the sort of place two friends would sit and share confidences. No dirty sniggers would be allowed in this place. And certainly, no men intimidating female customers, making asinine comments about how their own equipment and charm were far better than any vibrator.

A Woman's Pleasure. Focus on *woman*. Men were welcome, but Lily hoped the feel of the shop would put off those looking for a porno mag and quick jollies.

Anticipation thrummed in her belly. Starting from today, she was open for business. *Her* business, not beholden to anyone else. She didn't have to toe a company line, she *was* the company. Or rather, she was a sole trader. One side of her mouth quirked up. Even Bill Gates had started somewhere.

It was still early, so she went to the tiny space at the back of the shop and made coffee. She took the cup outside to feel the sun's warmth for a few minutes. Resting against the veranda post, she looked down the sloping street to the centre of Grasstree Flat. A steady stream of cars passed, and people stepped into the grocery store, or took coffee at one of the outside cafés. Saturday was market day and many people carried bags of dark green avocados or ripe tomatoes.

She switched her gaze from the bustling main street to rest on the shop next door. Which of the women she'd seen peering in her window was the owner? With luck, it was the one with the curly hair and wide smile. The other woman, the older one, had a sour cast to her, as if life was hard and the world was looking the other way. Maybe they ran it together.

It was nearly nine. Lily threw the dregs of her coffee—the strong, sweet espresso her Cuban father always drank—into a large planter. The flowers in it were wilting slightly; she'd water them later.

A click made her look up. The sour woman she'd seen yesterday opened the door of the adjoining shop and switched the sign to *Welcome, Friend*.

Lily took a couple of paces towards her. "Hi, I'm Lily. You must be my neighbour." She smiled and offered a hand. "I'm happy to meet you."

"Freya." She grunted the name, as if it were some secret code, shared reluctantly. She folded her arms. "What did you just empty into my flowers?"

Lily's hand hovered in the air and she withdrew it. "Just the dregs of coffee. I'll water them later."

"Don't touch them." Freya stalked over to the planters and peered suspiciously at the blooms, as if Lily had tipped weedkiller over them. "I'll care for my own plants."

"They're lovely." Lily offered a conciliatory smile. "I thought the council maintained them, as they're on the street."

"Mine." The word was clipped. "I take pride in *my* community."

Lily chose to ignore the faint stress on the *my*. "Mine too now. I'm looking forwards to life here, to the space and peace after where I've been living." It was an opening of sorts, designed to lead Freya into conversation. Most people would have responded with "Oh? Where did you live before here?" but Freya remained silent. Her nostrils flared slightly, as if she smelt something distasteful.

"I've come from Sydney. Newtown."

"Did you own the same sort of shop?" Freya's eyes were a piercing silver, and when she turned her gaze on Lily, it was as if she were pinned to the window behind.

"Yes. But A Woman's Pleasure is my shop. Before, I managed other people's."

"And you didn't stay somewhere that such a shop would be welcome?"

"Meaning the city?"

"Exactly."

She forced a smile onto her tight lips. "I hope my shop will be welcome here."

"It's not."

Tread softly, Lily. She's your neighbour. She's an arrogant bitch. She quashed the thought that jumped into her head. "Time will tell."

Freya sniffed. The morning sun turned her thin body into silhouette. Her wiry hair escaped the confines of the wide rag band she used to keep it off her face. Strands of grey made silver by the sun glinted as Freya turned on her heel and strode to her doorway. "And I don't appreciate you trying to connect your shop with mine."

"What do you mean?" Lily frowned. "We share a porch. That's not my doing."

"I mean the name. It's tacky. And it's obviously designed to make people think our shops are related."

13

Lily arched an eyebrow. The self-centredness of Freya's comment was mind-boggling. "It's nothing to do with you. My Australian Business Number is clearly displayed. Why don't you look it up? I've owned this business name for the last four years."

Freya pushed open her doors. Indian chimes tinkled a welcome. "I will." And she was gone, leaving Lily staring at the sign. Welcome, Friend indeed. She hoped Freya was nicer to her customers than she was to her.

Lily didn't expect to be busy, not on the first day, but she hoped for some curious passing trade. She expected some initial reluctance, but her research on Grasstree Flat told her this was the perfect little town. The population was younger than in many hinterland towns, a mix of commuters to the coast less than an hour away and the local alternative community. This sort of town, with its new-age energy and alternative vibe was perfect.

She just had to entice customers through the door.

Under the guise of putting out her chalkboard, she took a look up and down the street. A trickle of people were passing, but more people were bustling in and out of the naturopath, and the old-fashioned gentleman's outfitters in the main part of town. Lily put her board on the footpath. A bright sunflower and a flight of bluebirds shaped like an arrow pointed to her door with the words *Curious? Come and look.*

The Indian chimes on Freya's shop door tinkled. A young woman manoeuvred a baby stroller across the porch to the street. Lily smiled and stood aside to let her pass.

"Thanks," the woman said, and smiled in return. After her neighbour's snark and prickles, it was welcome.

Back inside her shop, Lily made another cup of coffee and took her tablet to one of the comfy chairs, where she could see if anyone entered. The document was still a jumble, but somewhere in the mishmash of words and ideas was the outline for a workshop. Sexual Fluidity. It was a topic close to her heart and was one that would hopefully be popular. Not immediately, but soon. She needed to get people comfortable with the idea of her and her shop before she could start her workshops. The outline took shape as she jotted some headings: *Comfortable in your skin. I am who I am. Sexual identity—why do I have to fit into a box?*

The buzzer on her door sounded, harsh and abrupt, so different to next door's chimes. Maybe she could get something softer too.

Three girls entered the shop, giggling and nudging each other. One darted to the nearest table. "Hey, Evelyn, look at this. What d'you reckon this is for?"

Lily frowned. Her first customers, and if her assessment was right, she was going to have to ask them to leave. Standing, she went over to them. "Hi, girls."

They looked up at her voice. Lily heaved a breath. If these three were older than sixteen, then she was a vicar's uncle. "Can I see some ID?"

"Left it at home." One, bolder than her friends, smirked as she looked Lily in the eye.

"All of you?"

"Yeah. Didn't think we'd need it. Everyone in town knows us." The second girl hung on to her friend's arm and giggled.

"Well, as you can tell, I'm new here, so I need to see some ID before I can let you in."

"Why?" The quietest of the three had a gentleness about her that her brash and sassy friends lacked. "We're only looking."

Lily softened her tone. "You need to be eighteen to come in here. State law."

"We're eighteen." It was Miss Bold again.

"Great. Then you're welcome to come back with your ID. But now I must ask you to leave." She crossed to the door and held it open.

For a moment, she thought they were going to refuse. But then the quiet girl tugged on Miss Bold's sleeve. "Come on, Ev. We better go."

The first two girls trooped out, ignoring Lily. The quiet girl slipped out after them. "Thanks," she said.

Lily nodded, and stood in the entrance, watching them make their way down the street in the direction of the market. For a moment, she thought about going next door, taking a look inside Freya's shop, but the memory of gimlet-sharp eyes and a clipped voice dissuaded her. There would be another chance, maybe at a better time.

The banging on the wall of her flat last night had probably been Freya. It made sense that she too lived above her shop. Lily had tapped the dividing wall after she'd turned the music off and been surprised at how thin it was. Maybe a single plank. No plasterboard, no insulation. No wonder her neighbour had been annoyed.

She went back inside and sat again, picking up the tablet. *Emotional needs and sexual needs: what if they're not satisfied by the same person?* That was a topic for later in the course. Maybe.

An image of Freya participating in such a course leapt into her head. Sitting on the beanbags and informal seating she preferred for such groups, laughing with other women, sharing stories. She shook her head. No, she couldn't imagine her neighbour attending.

Lily wrote for a while longer, but the empty shop yawned hollow and couldn't be ignored. She went to the window and twitched aside the dark curtain that shielded the interior from the outside. Two women stood and chatted in the street right outside her window. They didn't even glance her way.

Something was missing. Her chalkboard should have been exactly where the women were standing. Lily went to the door and looked out. The chalkboard was propped against the wall, the yellow sunflower and bluebirds facing inwards. The day was hot with not a breath of wind. It couldn't have blown over

She went outside, tossing a hello to the women on the pavement. She placed the chalkboard back where it would be seen, close to the women.

One of them looked at the sign. "I'll have to come in."

"Anytime." She didn't push it, just went back inside and left the door open.

Chapter 3

"THANKS, MOLLY." FREYA HANDED OVER the brown paper bag containing the smudge sticks. "I've included the instructions for use and a meditation that may be beneficial before you begin. *Namaste*." She turned to the woman waiting. "Jill, I'm happy you're here. Your book came in this morning." She reached under the counter and produced the Pilates book Jill had ordered.

"Thanks." Jill caressed its smooth cover. "I hope this will be helpful. Can I leave it on the counter whilst I look around? I'm after more candles. My bloody dog chewed up the coconut one I got last time. I said it smelt good; Bolto obviously agreed. I better go for something less appealing."

"Try something citrus. Dogs generally don't like that." Freya came around the counter and over to where the candles were. She plucked an orange blossom candle from the shelf and handed it to Jill.

"That's good."

"Or grapefruit."

Jill sniffed the wax of the second candle. "Heaven. If Bolto chews this, I'll slice him open to get it back."

Freya took both candles back to the counter and wrapped them in tissue paper.

Jill browsed her way along the rack of books, pulling out a couple to read the blurb before sliding them back. "Have you been in to the shop next door?" She turned to face Freya, a book on jewellery-making in her hands. "I thought at first it was connected to you... The name, y'know, but the lady in there says you're separate."

"We are. The name is just a coincidence." After her last exchange with Lily, she'd looked up Lily's ABN. Sure enough, A Woman's Pleasure had been registered to Lily Garcia for the last four years.

"They work well together." Jill returned to the counter and pulled out her credit card. "The shop is good. Tasteful, don't you think?"

Freya's lips thinned. "I wouldn't know." She pushed the card reader towards Jill. "I haven't been in."

She hadn't bumped into Lily either. The occasional snatch of song that drifted through the wall or an open window in the evenings had been subdued, as though the singer was now conscious of her neighbour and the thin party wall. Tension radiated through Freya's shoulders at the memory.

"You should." Jill continued, clearly oblivious to Freya's withdrawal. "It's welcoming. The owner is great. Very warm, but knowledgeable. Unembarrassable." She grinned. "I guess that last one's a plus in her industry."

Freya handed the card back. "It doesn't belong here, that shop. We're a small town, a close-knit community. That sort of thing belongs in the city."

Jill's brow arched up. "I think you'd be surprised, if you went in."

"I'm surprised the council let it through."

"It took a while. My hubby works in the council offices, and he said there were a couple of conditions, but the owner was easy to work with." She took the bag. "I'll leave you to it, but I'll see you later for yoga."

"No worries." Freya nodded and waited until Jill left before making a cup of spice tea. She needed the pick-me-up. Jill was the third customer in the last couple of days who had commented on the shop next door, and nearly all the comments had been positive. The only faintly condemning one had been from a schoolteacher, who mentioned that two of her students had boasted how they'd gone in. She had been about to quiz them on it, when their friend, quiet little Melissa, said the owner had asked them to leave. Nicely asked, she said.

It didn't fit with Freya's jaundiced view of sex shops and their predatory nature. She moved over to the wall that divided the shops. Most of it was covered with her displays, but if she pushed aside the hemp clothing, she could squeeze in alongside. She hesitated. What did she care what went on next door? But she did care, she acknowledged. She could justify that curiosity under the guise of gathering evidence to get the shop closed down.

Before she could talk herself out of it, she picked up a glass from the spring water fountain, and squeezed in behind the hemp jackets. From there, without the baffle of clothing, she could hear soft music. Something slow with a jazz vocal. Sensuous. The low buzz of voices filtered through, but she couldn't make out the words. She put the glass to the wall and pressed her ear to it.

Nothing. Just the same voices, a bit louder, but still no words. Freya lowered the glass and stood with her palm on the timber wall. Really, what was she thinking? Eavesdropping like a teenager spying on her parents. She turned, glass in hand, and pushed past the clothing again to come face-to-face with a couple staring at her.

She flushed but lifted her chin. "There's dry rot in that wall. I was checking the spread."

The couple eyed her askance but didn't comment, and after browsing half-heartedly through the pottery and cookware, they left without a backwards glance.

"… and into cat…" Freya, on all fours, arched her spine and dropped her head. "Tuck your tail bone underneath you. And now, back to cow." Her back hollowed and her chin came up.

She broke the pose and stood, casting a glance over her class. Most of the twelve or so women were regulars, well used to the poses. Carly, who seldom missed a class, grinned up at her from the front row. Her bright floral leggings and loose pink T-shirt stood out from the other women's more restrained garb.

Freya moved over to one of the two beginners. "That's it, Cass. Relax your shoulders and lower back." She placed a light hand on Cass's spine to demonstrate, nodding as the woman's body softened under her touch. Now her cow took on the sway-back posture of an old dairy cow.

The yoga room was bright with diffuse sunlight coming through the windows. Soft pan pipes played in the background. The humped backs of the women stretched out in hare pose made spots of colour on their yoga mats. Freya moved around the airy room, occasionally correcting a pose, sometimes returning to the front to demonstrate.

She let the class rise to their feet and led them in a series of lunges. Nobody talked; even the beginners knew these poses. Freya concentrated on her breath and awareness of her body, moving slowly, sensing the stretch and flex of muscles, the strength and flow of energy down through the soles of her bare feet. She focused on the present, breathing into it to anchor her awareness in the moment. The soft notes of the soundtrack resonated quietly. Freya stretched into an upwards salute.

There was a rattle, then a series of bangs as if someone were shaking a stuck door. Freya frowned and glanced at the two doors that led to the studio: one from her shop, one from the backyard. Another rattle, then a thump.

"Warrior pose," Freya said in a calm voice. "Focus on your breathing, on the position of your body."

A puff of dust and a few flakes of paint fell from the old painted door near the front of the room. A door that had never been used in the seven years Freya had operated A Woman's Spirit. Rusty hinges creaked, and then the door was flung open. Lily burst in as if she'd been shoved from behind.

She pivoted to face the room and her brows lifted as she took in the dozen women in leggings and oversize T-shirts now staring at her, their warrior poses in disarray.

"Hi," she said. "Sorry to interrupt. I thought I was fighting my way into a very stubborn closet." The comment appeared to amuse her for some reason; a grin formed and fled her face.

"There is a class in progress." Freya grated the words. "Please leave."

Lily's mouth opened again, and for a moment she seemed as though she would argue. Out of the corner of her eye, Freya could see her class had, as one, abandoned warrior pose—although in truth, to hold it this long required quads of steel, something few of them possessed—and were standing in relaxed positions. She caught a couple of smiles and nods of recognition directed at Lily.

Lily drew herself in. "Of course. My apologies for the unintended interruption." She disappeared back through the door to her shop and closed it gently behind her. Only dust and paint flakes remained to show where she'd been. But in Freya's head, she stood there still; a large, colourful woman, her dark hair scrunched on top of her head, a wide, easy smile that flashed white against her copper skin, and a blur of bright clothes. She left behind an aura of vitality and humour that reminded Freya of the tumble of music that had come through the wall. Freya's bare soles tingled. It was as if a flight of king parrots had wheeled through the room, all noise and disruption and garish colours, but still beautiful to see.

She turned back to her pupils. "Stand tall, ladies. Deep breaths in a four-seven-eight pattern..."

The Indian chimes tinkled a couple of hours later. Freya left the new stock she was unpacking and went to see to the customer. She frowned at the sight of Lily browsing along the teak tables and display shelves. She looked bigger amongst the small items Freya sold, tall and solid amongst delicate things. But her bright gauzy blouse could have come from Freya's own racks of clothing.

"Can I help you?"

Lily turned at Freya's voice and put down the brass candle snuffer she'd been holding. More like fondling it, Freya thought with a twist of anger. She'd been running a finger over its shiny surface, feeling the edge and curves of its shape.

"I'm sure you can." Lily advanced a pace. "I'm working on a schedule for my workshops. They don't require as much space as yours, but all the same, the studio at the rear of the shops is the best place to hold them." She picked up some tiny spice dishes made of bright pottery. "These are gorgeous. They remind me of my Cuban gran, my *nona*. She used dishes like this when she cooked. A pinch of this, a twist of that. I'll have to come back with my purse and get some." She stacked three non-matching dishes in a pile and smiled at Freya. "And actually, the studio is the only place for my classes. I can't run them in my shop. Not enough room. I'm going to start three, maybe four, classes each week, depending on demand, of course. But you were here first, so I'd like to fit in with your schedule."

"I beg your pardon?" Even in her own ears, Freya's voice sounded brittle, like stained glass crunching underfoot. "I'm sorry, but I'm not willing to rent you studio space. Even if I were, I don't think your classes would be an appropriate use."

Lily cocked her head to one side. "I don't get what you're saying. I don't need to rent it; that studio is on my lease, shared with you."

"You're wrong. I've leased my shop for seven years, and in all that time, that space has been mine alone. Diane, who had your shop previously, never used it."

"Maybe she didn't need to. The lease clearly states it's not for storage. Maybe she had no other reason to use it."

"There's nothing to talk about. You will have to find somewhere else." Freya turned away, her shoulders in a stiff set of dismissal. The Indian chimes tinkled. "Excuse me. I have to see to my customer."

She ignored Lily's bemused shrug and moved to greet the newcomer.

"I'll come around after closing time with my lease. Then we can work it out." Lily's tones were polite, but there was something unbreakable in her voice. As if she expected a battle.

Let her think that. Freya had battled before. She was no stranger to the combat between people. She had worn down officials, councillors, medics of all types. She had protested causes and signed petitions, donated and rallied, asked strangers for money, their time. Their caring. If Lily thought she could beat her down, she would soon learn.

In all of Freya's forty-one years on this earth, she had only lost one time.

Chapter 4

SWEETEN HER UP. THAT WOULD be the best approach. Wear her down with friendliness, wrap her with warmth. Bringing people around to your side was easier if you were nice to them. Rudeness never worked. Her new neighbour would do well to remember that, Lily thought with an inwards snort. Nona had taught her the value of being pleasant. Her *nona* had immigrated to Sydney from Cuba, and her stories of communities bound together by necessity and hardship still resonated with Lily. Nona's talk of growing veggies on rooftops, and informal community co-ops were part of the reason for Lily's decision to leave the big smoke and open her shop in a small town. Cuba's situation had been brought about by outside influences and a hand-to-mouth existence, but Nona's stories of the warmth of her small community were woven into the bright fabric of Lily's childhood. The doctor may not make house calls on a bicycle in Grasstree Flat, but Lily was sure the community would reach out to draw her in.

If she could get past Freya and her spiny exterior. What she'd already seen of the town, from her reconnaissance trips and since moving here, was a tightly knit community that was nevertheless warm and welcoming to newcomers. On her first visit, nearly a year ago, she'd sat outside a café on the main street enjoying some winter sunshine. The sweet-faced waitress had gone out of her way to figure out how to make a cuban espresso for Lily. Or as close to one as she could get. Lily had confided she was thinking of moving here, and the waitress's enthusiasm had been spontaneous and genuine.

Lily was sure she'd caught a glimpse of Freya at that same café in the past few days, chatting and laughing with the same waitress. It was a cosy picture, but it was hard to reconcile the relaxed and talkative Freya with the tense and aggressive one who always seemed to come out in Lily's presence.

But whatever she thought of Freya, they were neighbours. And unless Freya closed shop and moved away, they would be neighbours for the next three years at least—the length of Lily's current lease. And after that, if her instincts ran true. Grasstree Flat *felt* right. She'd fallen in love with it the first time she'd driven west from the coast, bursting out of the band of rainforest that covered the coastal hills to see the Pioneer River meandering through the wide, flat valley. The grasstrees that gave the town its name studded the drier north-facing slopes, like so many ragged explosions of green streamers. Even the subtropical humidity didn't seem too bad. She was comfortable here, tentatively reaching out to make friends. She wasn't one to be all woo-woo and into the cosmic vibrations of a place, but Grasstree Flat appealed to her in a way Sydney had lacked—at least for her. Grasstree Flat already was her town. She even hoped Nona would make the long trek from Sydney to pay her a visit.

Given that she intended on going nowhere, it would be far easier if she and Freya got along. Were friends, even.

The timer dinged, and she opened the ancient oven and pulled out the tray of oatmeal slice. She found a plate that didn't have too many chips and slid the slice onto it. If she were going to visit a friend, she'd take along a bottle of wine as well, but Freya was hardly a friend. Also, she didn't know if Freya drank alcohol. She was likely to consider Lily a lush as well as a purveyor of porn if she brought wine. With a longing glance at the small wine rack by the door, she descended the stairs to the entrance porch and hesitated. She wasn't sure how to reach Freya's flat. Whilst hers had a separate entrance, there was only the shop door on Freya's side. But to one side of the door—whose sign now said, *Namaste. Return Again, Friend*—there was a doorbell. She rang it and waited, staring idly out to the street. Two dogs trotted by and a car drove slowly past. She rang the bell again—maybe it wasn't working.

Or maybe Freya was ignoring her.

She stabbed the bell once more, pressing for a few seconds. Footsteps sounded and then the door jerked open.

"You're not in the city now. Not everything moves at your pace."

"May I come in?"

"I can't see that we have anything to say to each other. But if you insist." Freya turned and stalked through her shop to the rear, where a set of stairs led up.

That Freya's apartment was nothing like the woman herself, was Lily's first thought. If she'd been asked to speculate, she would have said that Freya would have chosen white walls and practical hessian floor coverings. Despite the profusion of gaiety and colour in Freya's shop, Lily had her pegged as an austere woman who probably made it a policy to own as little as possible: a large teak table maybe, practical hard chairs that were uncomfortable to sit on, and a small bookcase filled with worthy but dull titles.

The apartment, whilst a mirror of her own in layout, was painted in earth tones. The floor was polished boards—something deep and glowing chestnut—with the same rag rugs Lily had seen for sale downstairs. Lily skirted around two low couches and a coffee table piled high with magazines where a bottle of red wine was open and breathing. One wall was bare of furniture, but a sprawling hand-painted mural covered most of it. It was a fantastical world of curling vegetation and multiple suns, and two naked women walking hand in hand. She moved closer to examine it, but Freya's voice stopped her.

"Come out to the balcony." Freya threw open the doors, and Lily followed, stepping over a yoga mat placed on the polished boards.

"I made oatmeal slice for you."

Freya didn't even glance at it. "You shouldn't have gone to the trouble. I'm vegan."

Maybe this was an opening to soften this woman. "So am I. There's nothing in this we can't eat." She set the plate on the table in front of the couch and moved over to the railing. "I love sitting on my balcony in the evenings, watching the street, hearing the birds. But you've got the better view." Freya's balcony had the westerly aspect that hers lacked, and the sun slanted low, the heat blocked by a wall of green herbs growing in pots stacked high. She recognised rosemary, basil, parsley, marjoram, and sage, along with more unusual plants: mushroom plant, vietnamese mint, and some Lily didn't recognise.

Freya stood with her back to the street, arms folded, and pursed her lips.

"I brought the lease." Lily held it up. Freya didn't invite her to sit, so under the guise of spreading out the pages, she settled herself on the couch.

A tabby padded silently in and jumped up alongside Lily. "You beauty." She petted the soft fur, and the cat closed its eyes and purred. "What's her name?"

"Dorcas." The word was clipped, as if it were classified information.

"She's a darling."

Dorcas stepped daintily, one paw at a time, onto Lily's lap, turned around, and settled down. Freya's glare at her cat's defection could have singed Lily's hair.

Lily flicked the pages of the lease until she came to the relevant section. "Here. It says the area behind both shops is shared. No storage use permitted; the space is for occasional use as a studio, workshop, meeting space or similar." She held out the papers to Freya, who took them without a word.

"I'm going to run workshops on women's sexuality," Lily continued. "I hope they will assist women in expressing themselves. As young women. As mature women. I also want to help them with erotic expression, their sexual health, maximising pleasure—"

A snort from Freya. "You're promoting your own smutty goods."

"Don't knock what you haven't seen. You haven't set foot in my shop."

"I don't need to."

Lily heaved a breath. "Can we talk about this calmly? We share a space behind our shops. It would be good if we could do it amicably. Our businesses are not so dissimilar."

Freya folded her arms. "Our businesses have nothing in common. Nothing except a party wall."

"You're wrong. I've read your leaflets around town. You run yoga and meditation classes, workshops about empowering women to take control of their lives. About living life to the fullest, living productively and with satisfaction. I also came across a leaflet for your healthy living seminar and another on vegan cooking. I didn't realise you're a naturopath as well."

Freya nodded. She moved to sit at the far end of the couch from Lily, twisting her fingers in her lap.

Lily lifted her hands so Dorcas could switch laps, but the cat stayed put. "My seminars encourage women to embrace their sexuality. To take control of it, rather than leaving it in the hands of their partners... no pun intended. To accept where they fall in the gender and sexuality spectrum. I encourage women to reach their full potential, just as you do."

"I focus on strength. I teach women to rise above the physical, to become spiritual beings. Unlike you with your emphasis on their baser instincts."

"Is that what you think?" Lily's voice rose incredulously. "That sexual expression is somehow inferior?" Freya lifted her chin and silence was Lily's answer. "I need a glass of wine. I saw that bottle on your table. Right now, it would be neighbourly to offer me a glass."

"And prolong this inconvenience? I don't think so."

"We have complementary aims. Why can't you see that? When I signed the lease for my shop, I was so excited that you would be next door. I saw us working together, building our businesses alongside each other. My clients would be yours and vice versa—"

"What the hell were you smoking? That is not going to happen."

"What is your problem with sexuality? That's what all this comes down to, isn't it? You don't like sex. Fine. That's your choice, and none of my concern. However, as someone who encourages women to be what they want to be without censure or shame, I find it a strange stance."

"I'm not anti-sex. Why would I be? Many of my friends and customers are in relationships. But I encourage them to approach their relationships on an equal footing with their partner. There also comes a time in a woman's life when sex isn't so important. When it's a physical urge that can be overcome. Sex is basically an urge to procreate. Remove that urge and sex—"

"I disagree. Sex is intimacy, love, even. And yes, it's fun and exciting and a way of connecting with others, if that's what you want. It's not something to be shoved aside—unless it's the individual's choice and not foisted on that person by others or by society. I offer ways to enhance a physical relationship."

"And I offer ways to rise above it—*if that is the individual's choice*." Freya spat Lily's phrase back. "I don't rope my pupils like cattle and drag them through the door."

Lily took a breath, and relaxed her shoulders. Another, and her smile reappeared. "You're right. We both offer choices. The difference is, I'm not putting difficulties in the way of people wanting to follow your path. I don't tell my customers that the shop next door is a blight that should be banned."

At Freya's involuntary start, Lily continued, "Yes, I know you do that. Some of my customers are also yours. Is that so difficult to believe? I also don't take your signage off the street, and I'm not the one being difficult about the shared use of the studio. I'm offering to work around your established timetable even though I suspect that means you'll retain the most popular times."

Freya's crossed arms tightened against her body. The wall between them was mortared into place by their differences. Still,

Lily persisted. This wasn't just about her irascible, obstinate neighbour; this was about her business. Her workshops were an important part of her success or failure. The rear studio had been one reason she'd rented the shop. The real estate agent had told her the studio was there whilst showing her the shop. She'd been unable to view it as the door had been locked and the agent couldn't find a key, but he had told her it was a part of the lease.

"If you're unwilling to supply your timetable—well, I'll have to schedule my workshops as I see fit. If that clashes with one of your classes"—she shrugged—"we'll just have to share the space at the time. It will be a lot easier on both of us if you give me a copy of your timetable." She set Dorcas on the couch and stood. "We're not getting anywhere, which is a shame, as I don't want to fight with you." She glanced over to where Freya hunched on the couch. Her thin frame was tightened in on itself, as though she was cold, despite it being a warm spring day. Freya was an irritant that scratched her skin, like plunging through a thicket of lantana—defensive to the point of being impenetrable. But there must be more to her than she let Lily see. She had friends. She had pupils who attended her classes religiously. The woman must be doing something right.

"Enjoy the oatmeal slice. It's a recipe I was given by my meditation teacher." She paused for a moment, giving Freya an excuse to crack a smile, to invite her to sit awhile, have a cup of tea, share a piece of oatmeal slice. But her stony expression didn't change. "I'll see myself out."

She walked back through Freya's flat, over the polished boards, past the earth-toned walls. The mural again caught her eye. Animals peeped through jungle foliage; butterflies and vibrant birds were woven through the flowers. It was an

Australian rainforest with native flora and fauna, she realised. The painting faded at one end into an outline, as though the mural wasn't finished. She would have liked to stop and study it, but Freya obviously would not welcome that. And the two naked women, hand in hand. One of them looked not dissimilar to Freya herself. A bit younger, a bit plumper, not as sharp and diamond cut as the woman who even now was behind her. Doubtless to ensure she really did leave, Lily thought wryly, and that she didn't take the silverware with her.

"My class schedule is on the noticeboard in the yoga studio." Freya's voice was flat, as though she wasn't interested in Lily's response.

"Thanks. I'll take a look and let you know what I come up with."

She left.

Chapter 5

SEVEN WOMEN FILED OUT OF the studio at the end of Freya's Expressions Through Writing: Understanding Yourself Through Diarising workshop. They clutched pens and legal pads, leather-bound journals, bright cloth-covered notebooks, and even, in Marilyn's case, a pad of blank sheet music. She said the music lines helped inspire her.

Freya put down her own diary—a simple spiral-bound notebook—and stacked the chairs and small tables the class used. Everyone had left except for Karin, who was browsing the noticeboard, and Carly, whom Freya always had coffee with after the morning class.

Karin jotted something from the noticeboard in the back of her notebook. "This is new," she said. "Different for Grasstree Flat." She pointed to a flyer Freya hadn't seen before, which was jumbled in amongst the leaflets for market days, crystal healing, and chooks for sale. The flyer was bright and direct:

> Explore your feminine sexuality in a safe and non-judgmental environment. Sex and sexuality are shrouded in myths. Your doctor may be too

clinical. You may not feel comfortable discussing this with your friends. This workshop aims to demystify female sexuality in an open and relaxed manner. Learn about anatomy, pleasure, and the normality of sex. Improve your verbal and non-verbal communication skills to better receive what you want in the bedroom. All orientations welcome. Participate as much or as little as you want. No under-18s. No nudity and no intimate touching.

The banner at the top proclaimed *A Woman's Pleasure*. That shop again. Freya's nails dug into her palms. She'd had less irritation from a run-in with a stinging tree. What good could possibly come out of a class like this? And how dare Lily put it up without checking with her first. She reached for the flyer and pulled it from the board.

"Hey, if you're going to throw that, I'll have it." Karin held out a hand. "I think that would be good to go to. Maybe someone else I know as well. She's always complaining she doesn't know how to tell her husband what she really wants."

"I wanted a better look." The lie grated, but Freya made a point of smoothing out the crumpled paper, studying it, and then pinning it back on the board.

At least Lily had scheduled it for when Freya didn't have a class. Small mercy indeed.

The morning class finished at eight. Freya locked the shop and walked with Carly the short distance to the Green House, an organic café run by one of the women who attended Freya's evening yoga class. Remy acknowledged them with a lift of her hand, and they went to their usual table out front, shaded from the morning sun.

Carly studied the menu, even though she must know it by heart. "I'll have the brekky wrap. You?"

"Chia-and-pecan porridge."

"You always have that." Carly set the menu down and touched Freya's hand. "Change is good, you know."

"Says the person who *always* has the brekky wrap. I like the porridge, and it's the healthiest option."

Carly's blue eyes studied her. Freya could feel her pierce the layers of irritation and bad humour that had shrouded her in the weeks that Lily had been next door.

"You're not yourself these days, Frey. Want to tell me what's wrong?"

Those eyes wouldn't let up. Carly's gaze was intent on her face, her frivolous light-hearted demeanour vanished.

"Hey." Carly touched the back of Freya's hand, her fingers warm. "You can talk to me. You always used to."

Freya took a spoon from the cutlery holder in the middle of the table, placed it down in front of her, and handed a knife and fork to Carly, who took them without comment. The action bought her maybe thirty extra seconds.

"Nothing's wrong." She couldn't meet those steady blue eyes. "Okay, there is something. That woman next door."

"Lily?"

"Yes. She thinks we run similar businesses. Ha! The only similar thing is that our shops are mirror image. She sells tacky porn. She's brash. She intrudes upon my space." Freya broke off as Remy brought their usual coffees, and took their brekky orders. As she walked away, Freya continued. "Now she wants studio time. It's in her lease."

Carly's forehead wrinkled. "I thought that was your space."

"So did I. But it's there in black and white. I guess because Diane never used it, I made the assumption."

"What does she want to do?"

"Sex classes. Did you see her flyer on the noticeboard?" Freya shut her lips with a snap. Even the soy latte steaming in front of her didn't appeal at that moment.

"No. But I've heard from Janie there were classes starting in town. These must be the ones she was talking about. They sound interesting. Confronting for some, maybe, but those people won't go along."

"She's promoting the sex toys in her shop."

"Do you know that or are you assuming?" Carly broke eye contact and took a sip of her coffee. "I thought I might go."

"Why?"

"Because my sex life could be a lot fucking better—pun intended. And nothing I do seems to make any difference. Andy still rolls on, pumps away, and rolls off. Oh sure, he kisses me, sucks my nipples, delves around and rubs where he thinks my clit is. If Lily's workshop can help improve upon that, it's money well spent."

"But a *sex* class?"

"We're not all like you, Frey. I *like* sex. I like the closeness and intimacy—even when Andy's being a dickhead, it still makes things better. You don't seem to need it anymore... But..." She reached a hand across the table and rested it on Freya's. "It's been three years since Sarah died."

"And that time is supposed to turn me into a sex machine? I'm now supposed to want casual sex with other women? Are you saying I should come along to this class because I need it?" Her gaze skittered down Grasstree Flat's main street, up to where the clouds scudded along in the blue, blue sky. Anywhere other than at the well-meaning concern on Carly's face.

"No, of course not. But it would be a start. It's not just about sex. It's about intimacy. Emotional fortitude." She fiddled with the packets of sugar as though the action gave her courage. "I've barely heard you mention her name in three years. Sarah was my friend as well as your partner. I miss her too."

"Are you saying I need a psychologist?"

Carly's silence dragged on.

"Well?" She beat a tattoo on the inside of the mug with the teaspoon as she stirred her coffee.

"I can't answer that. You know I can't. But I don't think it would hurt to let people in a little more. You can talk to me anytime. I cared about Sarah and I care about you."

Remy returned with their breakfasts and set them down. "I don't need to ask who has what. You're both as predictable as the sunrise." She glanced between their two set faces. "Am I interrupting something?"

"No." Freya's expression was 80 percent grimace. "Carly's finished trying to persuade me to attend the sex class run by the shop next door."

"Did she succeed? If so, I'll see you there. I'm going." Remy sat in the vacant chair.

"You don't have a partner. Neither do I. Sex isn't a part of our lives."

"Speak for yourself. I'm old, not dead, and I'm a master of solo sex, if you know what I mean." Remy winked. "I might learn some new tricks."

"I'm not going. And I'm surprised the two of you are. I thought we were above all of the physical excesses." Freya's mouth snapped shut.

"You may strive for that." Carly's words were as gentle as the thumb that stroked the back of Freya's hand. "I don't."

Remy nodded her agreement.

"Then why do you both come to my classes?" Warmth and support rolled in waves from her friends, but despite that, betrayal settled in her gut. Friends supported each other unconditionally. Didn't they?

"Because you teach good living, physical wellbeing, how to look after your body. I love yoga. It makes me feel good, gives this flabby old body some tone." Remy leant forwards. "But everything in moderation. I take what I need from your classes. I'll take what I need from Lily's class too. Attending a sex class isn't going to turn me into Madonna."

A snort from Carly. "I hope *not*."

"Hey, I'm a fan of Madge! She was my idol when I was growing up. I wanted to be just like her, conical breasts and all." The bell at the counter dinged, and Remy rose. "Gotta run. See you both at Lily's sex class."

Carly cut into her brekky wrap, wiped a finger in the oozing barbeque sauce, and licked it. "Well? Will you come?"

"No." Freya took a spoonful of porridge and blew on it.

"Just no? No reason, no room for persuasion? I won't leave your side. And if you want to leave, you say and I'll leave with you. No questions."

"No. Just no." How to explain to Carly that even the thought of it made her tighten with anxiety? Talking sex. With strangers. And even worse, with *that* woman. How to explain that just seeing her neighbour, bouncing through life with her bold figure, garish colours, too-loud laugh and too-wide smile made her want to retreat from the brashness? Carly might suggest forging common ground with Lily, but Freya couldn't imagine Lily meditating or reading, or seeking a spiritual path. Everything that was important in her own life.

Lily. Even the name was light and bright, no weight or depth to it. She glanced across at Carly. Everything she'd just thought about Lily applied to Carly too. Yet Carly was her friend. Maybe her closest friend. She'd been there for her, a solid, supportive figure, when Sarah died. Had Freya been the sobbing, wailing type, she had no doubt Carly's shoulder would have been there for her. Carly would have done anything Freya asked if it had lessened her grief.

She turned her attention back to the present, the here and now: this café, this breakfast with a friend, this sunshine glinting on the road, this town, the birds, the sky, the red car driving down the street. She looked at Carly's down-bent head as her friend cut into her brekky wrap. Carly's earlier words came back to her along with the despondency in her normally upbeat friend's voice when she'd briefly mentioned her sex life.

Freya's mouth thinned. Andy wasn't the worst bloke around; genial enough, pleasant to her. But Carly's comments about her sex life hadn't painted that picture. Freya mentally kicked herself. For someone supposedly so in tune with her friends, someone who prided herself on supporting her women friends, she'd missed these little signals.

"Is everything all right with you and Andy?"

Carly's head came up, startled, and she blinked at Freya. "What made you ask that now?"

Freya shrugged. "Your tone of voice when you talked about your sex life. I'm sorry, Carly, I'm being an inattentive friend. I've been so caught up in that woman next door, I've been neglecting you." She rested a hand on Carly's. "Talk to me."

Carly put down her fork and reached for her coffee. "The usual, I guess. Andy's never been the most demonstrative of blokes, but he seems even more offhand than usual. Works late, but gets annoyed if I'm not home in the day when he calls."

Unease for her friend tickled fingers into Freya's mind. "What does he do when you're not there?"

Carly took her time answering. "Calls my mobile, of course. It's why mobile phones were invented, isn't it? Anybody you want at the touch of a button. But he always asks where I am and why I'm not at home."

"Tell him the fifties called and they want their gender roles back."

A smile flickered, then fled Carly's face. "Yeah. It's not like that, though." She heaved a breath and blew it out. "You know we're trying to get pregnant, right?"

Freya nodded.

"It's not working and it's been nearly a year. We've started putting money aside for IVF. So if ever he calls and I'm not home, he wants to know where I am and drills me on what I'm spending." She tilted her head at the table. "I tell him we just have coffee. He'd crack the shits if he thought I was wasting money on breakfast."

Freya chose her words with care. "He can't expect you to sit at home, surely?"

"No." Carly drew the word out. "But he lectures me about money—not that I spend much at all. Breakfast with you. Yoga classes. Food shopping. That's all."

"You have as much right to the money as he does."

"Yes, and he never used to be like this. It's only since we've started saving for IVF. It's expensive and our health insurance doesn't cover it. But hey, we're eating healthy. Veggies are cheaper."

"You don't have to pay for yoga. I know you turned down that offer once before, but I'm repeating it."

"No." Carly's eyes flashed. "It's your business. Friends are friends, but it's your livelihood. I pay you, just as I pay Remy for this brekky wrap."

"The needs of a friend take precedence over business. Come for free now. Then when you're pregnant you can start paying again."

"No, really, that's not fair. What if in twenty years' time I'm a permanent fixture on the IVF program?"

"Then I'd hope they'd give you mates' rates."

Carly snorted. "Maybe they have a loyalty card." She touched Freya's hand. "Thanks for talking. You're a good friend." She picked up her fork again and resumed eating. "Enough about me. I'm learning to cook, now that we're saving money. Care to share some of your vegan recipes? Anything tasty, as long as it doesn't include tofu."

"Lily's vegan." The words came unbidden, the memory of Lily's smile as she proffered the plate of her oatmeal slice flashing in her mind. She'd shunned it at the time, but she'd had a piece later with a cup of tea. It had been surprisingly good.

"See, she's not all bad. Maybe you'll end up best mates, and you'll remove the lattice between your balconies and host dinner parties together."

"Right. And maybe Grasstree Flat will become the centre of the civilised world."

"I thought it already was. But you could give Lily a chance."

Freya broke eye contact and gazed down the street. She had no room in her life for a woman like Lily. No room for her warm brown skin, her expressive eyes and wide smile. No room for her voluptuous figure, her loud clothes that drew attention to her curvy shape. Her vivacious, energetic presence.

No. She had no room for Lily in her life.

Chapter 6

THE WOMAN WAS IMPOSSIBLE. UTTERLY cantankerous; a skinny string of bad-tempered misery. Not just a roadblock to her enjoyment of life in Grasstree Flat, but a wall that stretched as tall as it was wide. Freya was spying on her. There was no other explanation. Whenever Lily watered her tomato plants, Freya shook the lattice between their balconies and snarled that Lily was wetting her chairs—chairs Lily was positive hadn't been there the day before. If she turned her music above a whisper, Freya banged on the wall for her to turn it down. She'd left a note on Lily's car one morning accusing Lily of sabotaging her trade by not allowing her customers to park out front of the shop. The fact there were acres of street parking on either side of Lily's small yellow car was apparently nothing to do with it.

Lily wasn't deliberately trying to antagonise her neighbour; on the contrary, she was going out of her way to smooth the path. She'd copied down the timetable pinned to the noticeboard in the studio, and arranged three classes of her own at times when the studio was vacant. Lily had left a note for Freya advising her of the times, and when she'd heard nothing after a couple of days, she'd made up flyers and posted them around town, including several on the noticeboard in the shared studio.

Then a terse note appeared under her door one morning, advising her that the early evening class she had scheduled for Tuesdays wasn't acceptable as Freya ran a seniors' yoga class that day. The note said it was a closed class and therefore wasn't included on the timetable. She gave no apology for the inconvenience of the late notification, just the short unsigned note penned in a small, closed-in script.

Lily set her jaw, moved her class, and sent back a polite note thanking Freya for the notification and asking if she had any more classes not on the general schedule.

Her only answer was silence.

Lily sat on the couch on her balcony, feet up on the low table, sipping a glass of wine. Dorcas purred like a lawnmower in her lap. Lily stroked the cat from the top of her contented head down over her tea-cosy body to the base of her tail. Dorcas rumbled louder. Any second now, Lily expected Freya to tear down the flimsy lattice to accuse her of stealing her cat. It wasn't her fault Dorcas came visiting, stalking daintily along the balcony railing to accept head rubs and pets from Lily.

But the adjoining flat was quiet. It was early evening. The sun still cleared the trees down the street, and a flock of rainbow lorikeets made their usual evening racket. A car door slammed, and two women in yoga pants and tunics walked towards the shared porch. Lily picked up the timetable that had so annoyed her. Ah yes, tonight was a beginners' yoga class. One hour, all welcome. First class free.

Lily put down her glass. What if she went to that class? She had time right now to go inside, find a pair of leggings and a loose T-shirt, and go down and join the group. Freya could hardly throw her out, and maybe she would see it as a gesture of conciliation. Maybe.

Decision made, she tipped Dorcas from her lap and rose from the couch. Dorcas watched her in mute affront for a moment before, disdainful of the drop, she paraded back along the rail to Freya's flat. Lily padded barefoot into her bedroom. Sure enough, at the back of the wardrobe was a haphazard jumble of her old yoga clothes. She selected a pair of bright orange leggings. They would do fine. She paired them with a lime T-shirt and leaving her feet bare, she bounded down the stairs.

The door to Freya's shop was now closed and it would be rude to barge into the studio through the door from her own shop a second time, so she walked around to the rear laneway, where the gate to the small yard stood open. Lily went through to the door that led into the studio. Soft music played, not so much a tune as a collection of chords and long notes designed, Lily supposed, to soothe and focus the mind. The class was underway. A dozen women sat in the easy pose of happiness. From the rear, she saw only their upright spines and shoulders and heard the slow susurration of their breathing.

"...bring in the awareness of your breath. Each inhale sends a wave of energy down your spine, deep into your hips, down, far into the earth beneath you." Freya spoke in a calming monotone. She didn't open her eyes when Lily entered.

Lily looked around, realising she should have brought a mat, although she wasn't sure if she still owned one or where it was. But she spied a loose pile of mats in one corner and snagged the top one. She took a place at the rear of the class and copied the pose of the woman next to her. Closing her eyes, she concentrated on her breathing and on the slow sound of Freya's voice.

"Imagine the sky energy pulling you upwards. Your body is light, your neck is lengthening. Relax your shoulders, rest here for several breaths. You are here, in the moment; let your body quieten from your day."

Freya's voice drifted away, and the studio was filled only with the sound of rhythmic exhales and the slow chords of music. She led the class through a series of gentle poses. Lily let her body and mind sink down through the layers of the day to find the stillness within. Irritations dissipated until nothing existed but her body, this warm room, and the gentle movement of air from the ceiling fan.

Freya's voice was closer now. Lily opened her eyes to see Freya walking soundlessly through the women, touching them with small movements to encourage them to soften a pose, let go of tension. Freya turned, and her eyes connected with Lily's. The jolt that ran through Lily was surely from the crackling antagonism emanating from the other woman. The flash of irritation, swiftly veiled, from those clear grey eyes was at odds with the soft tone of her voice as she touched a pupil's shoulder. *Relax*, the hand gesture said, but as her eyes locked with Lily's, the blaze burned for a fractured second before Freya closed her eyes and exhaled a long, slow breath. When she opened them, the fire was gone. Freya looked at her unsmiling, but she gave the smallest nod of... recognition, acknowledgment maybe. And there in the air a faint scent of something fresh. Sandalwood or rosemary. A hint of peppermint.

Freya moved on and Lily felt her absence keenly. Not just the lack of her scent, but the absence of *her*. And, too, a lessening of static, of the fine-spun tension. Lily envied that pupil, with Freya's hand on her, a gentle weight.

Lily didn't hang around at the end the class. Really, what was there to say? She slipped back through the door to her own shop before Freya could detain her.

The class had been pleasurable. She hadn't attended a yoga class in months, and she'd forgotten the joy of movement, of feeling her body stretch and flex. She made a simple salad for dinner, and as she ate it, she studied the studio timetable. That same class was held again in three days' time on Thursdays. She resolved to attend.

Lily again slipped into the Thursday class at the last minute. She took her place at the back and nodded to the woman next to her.

"Welcome, friends." Freya bowed over prayerful hands, and the class started. Lily focused on her body, the moment, the silent space inside her head, but even so, as soon as Freya walked amongst the pupils, placing a light hand to encourage or correct, Lily lost the focus on her inner self. Her breathing grew shallow with the tension in her chest. When Freya moved on without correction, only a quiet "Good" and a light touch on her shoulder, a vague feeling of disappointment formed and fled. Her shoulder was warm from Freya's brief touch, and a wave of positive energy seemed to flow from it down to her core.

Lily moved into warrior pose with the rest of the class, and her thigh trembled, unused to the position. Freya returned to the front of the class and moved into warrior pose with a steely grace. She was contained in her body, economical in her movements.

At the end of the class, Lily put away her mat and approached the front of the room, where Freya was chatting with one of the pupils. It was the woman Lily had seen her with the first day they'd met, the one with curly hair and an open, eager expression. Freya's grey eyes—no longer calm and peaceful, flashed silver daggers in Lily's direction at the interruption.

Lily placed her palms together. "*Namaste*. I enjoyed the class. I need to pay you."

"Twenty-five dollars."

Lily reached for the notes she had pushed into her pocket earlier. "Thank you. Is it okay if I keep attending?"

"Of course." The tone was far from warm, but the civility was a start.

"Tell her about the advance payment discount," the other woman prompted. She turned to Lily without waiting for Freya's response. "Pay ahead and get ten classes for two hundred bucks. It's a good deal if you intend to keep coming."

"I do. I'll do that next time." She looked directly into Freya's eyes. "I enjoyed your teaching."

"Have you done yoga before?" The curly-headed woman propped her backside against the desk.

"A long time ago. But it's amazing how quickly it comes back."

"I was the same. I used to do yoga when I was idealistic in my early twenties. Then I got married and somehow amongst all the trivia of everyday life, I lost the habit. Thanks to Freya, I'm back."

"That's good. I'm hoping to get back into the habit as well."

"Carly." She stuck out a hand, and Lily shook her damp palm. "I know you're Lily. I've signed up for your sexuality class starting soon."

"I'm glad to hear it. I hope you'll enjoy it."

"Oh, I'll enjoy all right. I need something like that." A sideways glance. "I'm trying to persuade Freya to come with me."

49

Freya shifted her feet, a side-to-side movement. "I've already said no, Carly. It's not for me."

Lily tilted her head on one side, and studied her. Freya's salt-and-pepper hair stuck out in a wiry mass on either side of her head. Freya was not attractive, not in a conventional sense. She was too thin, too tense, too wiry, too antagonistic, too combative. She was just too, *too*, Lily thought in amusement. But the memory of Freya's small, light palm touching her shoulder burned warm.

"Come along if you want. First class free. After all, that's what you offer. Then, if you don't like it, you don't need to return."

"Does that apply to me as well?" Carly's eagerness reminded Lily of a puppy: bouncy and cheery.

"Of course. And if you bring a friend"—she indicated Freya with a nod— "to the first class, you get the second one free as well."

"C'mon, Frey." Carly punched her friend lightly on the arm. "Do it for me."

Freya's face was already set in the blank wall of refusal. Conversation closed.

Lily jumped in before she could think better of it. "Actually, I was going to invite you to dinner." Where had those words come from and what had she just done? Set herself up for a tortured night of stilted conversation probably, but she couldn't go back now. The surprise on Freya's face was worth it. "So that we can get to know each other better as neighbours." She turned to Carly. "You're invited too, of course."

"I'd love to come. It will be good to see what you've done with the flat. Those apartments are lovely. High ceilings and so spacious."

"You'll be disappointed. I haven't done much. No time."
Her thoughts flicked to the mural on Freya's wall. Somehow,
she thought Freya had probably painted it herself. "How about
Sunday night? Will that work for both of you?"

"Fine for me." Carly nodded so hard, her curls bounced.
"Frey?"

"I'm not sure—"

"C'mon. You never do anything on Sundays." She turned
back to Lily. "I'll bring wine. If Freya snaps out of her stupor,
she'll bring nibbles."

"That sounds perfect." Deliberately, Lily didn't look at
Freya in case it gave her the motivation to refuse. "Seven?"

"That's good. We'll see you then."

It was the opportune time to leave. She lifted a hand in
farewell, and slipped through the door back to her own shop.
Freya for dinner. It could be interesting.

"I'm wheat-free as well as vegan." The reluctant words
followed her through the doorway. Freya could have been
talking about a visit to the dentist. "I don't eat much sugar."

Lily paused, and turned back to the studio. "That's no
problem. I'm sure I'll cope." She was coming. Lily had expected
this to be a duty invitation, but instead she found she was
looking forwards to it. Freya challenged her. She wanted to
find out what was behind her prickly exterior. Was she like an
echidna, all spines and snout, and then inside a soft little ball?
Carly too. Her chipper personality would make for entertaining
company. "I'll see you both on Sunday."

Chapter 7

SUNDAY PASSED SLOWLY. FREYA STARTED the day with her usual meditation, some stretching, went for a walk, and made a desultory attempt at housework. But somehow her soothing routines failed to have the desired effect. Instead of the usual methodology of cleaning, she found herself flitting from room to room. She stripped the bed, but then moved to the kitchen to make a cup of tea instead of putting fresh sheets on the mattress and cleaning the shower.

Dorcas followed her meowing until Freya picked her up, and the cat settled into her favourite position: across one of Freya's shoulders, her front paws hooked into the back of Freya's T-shirt.

Freya paced over to the doors leading to the balcony. She stared at a dead scarab on its back in the corner, at the drift of cobwebs above the glass. She should get the broom, dust over the coffee table, damp-mop the floors, water her plants. Instead her gaze wandered out through the glass and across to the hills on the other side of the valley. Her stomach jumped, and her grip tightened on Dorcas enough that the cat meowed in protest and her claws dug into Freya's shoulder. She drew a slow breath, trying to regain the equilibrium that had fled with Lily's invitation.

Instead of a time of peaceful solitude, the end of the day loomed large. Dinner with Lily. And Carly, although that barely made it past the perimeter of her mind. After all, she saw Carly often enough in the week that it was commonplace. Dinner with Lily certainly wasn't.

She tipped Dorcas onto the couch, and the cat glared in affront. But when Freya's bottom followed her down, Dorcas was appeased and tiptoed over to curl onto her lap, purring appreciatively.

What was she thinking?

Why had she agreed?

She should have shut the conversation down with an abrupt no. After all, she had nothing in common with Lily, and the woman was a living, breathing affront to Freya's own lifestyle. Just because Lily turned out to be vegan and now attended yoga, didn't make her any more likely to be a friend.

But, a tiny voice whispered in Freya's head, it should do. She stroked Dorcas absently, three fingers from between the cat's pointy ears down to the base of her tail. She'd watched Lily in the last yoga class. It was impossible not to. Wearing a bright pair of yellow leggings and a blue-and-white patterned T-shirt, she had moved through the poses with a certain amount of hesitation. But whilst she wasn't graceful, it had obviously not been her first time in a yoga class. Her movements grew surer as the class progressed, as though the muscle memory of poses was returning. And her face... It had been hard not to watch her, to see the calmness that stole over her face. Freya had sensed Lily sinking into herself, becoming absorbed in the movement and the quiet mind space. And then, at the end of the class, the final *namaste*, Lily's eyes had crinkled with the joy of her smile, and the sunshine and good humour emanating from that bright, big figure had spread in concentric circles from her still body.

Lily radiated pleasure and that was compelling.

Like Sarah, a tiny voice whispered in her head. Always living in the moment, taking the most pleasure from any situation.

Carly gravitated towards Lily; other friends, such as Remy, talked about attending her workshops. But the pull Lily exerted so effortlessly attracted followers. Freya felt the tug of it, like the tide, sucking away the sand from under her bare feet.

She shuffled around on the couch and tucked her feet underneath her. Dorcas mewed in protest but settled down again. Now Freya faced the opposite wall, where the mural dominated the room. Idly, her gaze traced the brushstrokes, the wisps of colour streaking the rainforest flowers, the curious stance of a wallaby half-hidden by a curling vine. And then, near the end of the mural, the naked figures, hand in hand. Herself and Sarah.

She'd seen Lily staring at the mural. Had Lily realised one of the figures was Freya? Had she wondered who the other woman was? Freya snorted. Many people had seen the mural in the years since she'd started it. Friends, family, acquaintances. But their glances had been uncomfortable and polite, their sliding-away expressions accompanying their stilted words of comfort. Few people studied it openly, as to do that raised Sarah's presence in the room, led to the necessity of talking about her. *Move on*, was in their awkward expressions. *Find someone new.* But Lily had studied the mural openly, with appreciation.

"You miss Sarah too, don't you, Dorcas?" The cat purred harder. The gentle vibrations were comforting.

She should finish the mural. Carly, one of the few people brave enough to mention Sarah to Freya, had suggested that doing so might bring closure. But Carly had said that in a diffident tone of voice, as if she didn't have the conviction of her words. "Maybe," Freya had responded, and she must have been off-putting; Carly had never mentioned it again.

Freya drew in a calming breath and focused on the two figures on the wall. Sarah's smile and joy were there, her painted face alive in the way Freya remembered. The brushwork was amateurish, but love brought out the emotion in her work.

"I love you, Sarah." She said the words aloud to the room, and sat for a few minutes longer, gathering her strength around her. Dorcas yawned and rolled over in her lap, baring her soft-furred tummy for Freya's touch.

After a few minutes, Freya set Dorcas gently to one side and went into the kitchen. Carly had told her to bring nibbles. Not doing so would be impolite. And she knew that Carly was hoping she would make her rosemary biscuits and pumpkin-and-cashew-nut dip. She filled a glass from the water purifier, and set about baking.

Freya waited until she heard Carly's voice through the thin wall rising and falling in animated conversation. Only then did she go and knock on Lily's door.

"It's open, come in!" Lily called down from above.

Freya looked around Lily's flat, eyeing the chaotic mess. Paperbacks lay in a toppling pile on the coffee table, and trailing green plants drooped over every shelf. Lily had placed low bookshelves along the party wall—the wall where Freya's mural was—and the books were stacked haphazardly on their sides, or crammed into the shelves. A slouchy couch had an inviting pile of cushions with bright designs. Although when she looked closer, those designs were abstract depictions of female genitalia. Freya tightened her lips; such overt display was unnecessary. She focused instead on the double french doors which were open to the balcony from where the warm air of a spring evening wafted in, aided by the ceiling fan.

Carly came up and hugged her, the tumbler of wine she carried coming precariously close to spilling.

"Hi." Lily stood in the doorway that led out to the balcony. With the light behind her, Freya saw only her silhouette and the swoop of her hair, hanging loose for once and breaking on her shoulders. Then Lily came forwards and her face came into view, graced by a smile.

An attractive face. Freya instantly set the thought aside. That was irrelevant. She handed Lily the plate of rosemary biscuits and the pumpkin-and-cashew-nut dip.

"These look delicious. Thank you." Lily gestured to the balcony. "We're out here. It's such a glorious time of day to be outside, and the view is so pleasant." She smiled. "But of course you know that. Forgive me, I don't mean to be patronising; most of my visitors haven't been here before. I'm not sure what you like to drink. I can offer wine, beer, tea, coffee, or mineral water."

The moral high ground of mineral water was tempting, but the wine was appealing. Lily had gone out of her way to be pleasant. The least she could do was reciprocate. She inclined her head at the tumbler on the table. "Some of that red wine would be good, if you have any left."

"I do." Lily disappeared towards the kitchen.

Left alone together, Carly grinned. "I'm glad you're here, Frey. Glad, too, you're relaxed enough to drink wine."

She contented herself with a small smile and moved to the table where Lily had set her nibbles. "I made your favourite."

Carly fell on the plate with a squeal of delight, and had eaten three of the rosemary biscuits by the time Lily returned with a tumbler of wine and handed it to Freya.

"Thanks." Freya sipped and was pleasantly surprised by the rich robustness. "This is lovely."

"Thanks. A friend moved to Margaret River in Western Australia and now works in a winery. She sent me a mixed case as a gift."

"Good gift." Freya took another sip. The wine rolled over her tongue in a blend of flavour.

"She's a good friend."

For a moment, a fleeting mist passed over Lily's face, replacing her habitual half smile. Freya caught her breath. Sadness. That's what it was. The familiarity of that emotion washed over her, and for a moment, a kindred connection twisted between them. Freya's hand reached towards Lily's and hovered, a second away from a comforting touch.

Carly hiccupped, an abrupt sound in the silence that hung in the room. "Sorry." She set her tumbler down on the table and hiccupped again. "Guess I drank that first glass a little too fast. Haven't eaten much all day and it's gone to my head."

"Eat more." Freya picked up the plate of biscuits and thrust it towards Carly, glad to have something to do with her hands. Her fingers tingled.

"I'm a bad hostess. I'll get you some water." Lily disappeared and returned in a moment with a glass.

"It really is good wine." Carly's irrepressible personality bounced back. "But I'll go easy, I promise. At least I live close enough to walk home."

"What's the name of the winery?" Freya asked.

Lily reached for the bottle, which was nearly empty. "Crimson Creek," she said, and passed the bottle to Freya. "My friend, Inga, designed the label. That's how she got to know the owner. And now she lives there. Guess love can coexist with business."

Once again, the fleeting shadow crossed her face.

"Where did she move from?" Carly sipped her water and helped herself to some of the dip, heaping it on a rosemary biscuit.

"Sydney." Lily shut her mouth abruptly.

"So you knew her in Sydney?" Carly persisted.

"She was my partner."

"Is that why you moved up here? Because your business partner dissolved the partnership in Sydney?"

It must be the wine, Freya thought. Carly wasn't normally this obtuse.

"Partly. But Inga and I were civil partners as well as business partners. I thought we had it good, but then Inga got the contract for the winery's advertising and fell in love with the owner, Cait." Lily shrugged. "Inga fell heavily and instantly in love. It took Cait a little longer to reciprocate—partly because she knew that Inga had a wife: me."

"Oh." Carly caught on in a rush. "I didn't realise you were married. I'm sorry."

"That's okay. Inga and I remained friends." Lily lifted her tumbler. "Hence this wine. She sends me a case every now and then. I'm an early taste tester."

"It tastes perfectly good to me." Carly winked.

Freya studied the dark red liquid in her glass. The wine was magnificent. The thought slid through her head that it was magnificent, too, that Lily had had a wife. Had. Loved and lost. Just as she had. Her lips thinned. *Not* as she had. Lily had had a wife who had left her for another woman. She'd had a wife who… No. Not the same at all.

"I'll leave the bottle. Let me check on dinner." Lily disappeared, leaving Freya and Carly alone.

"She's gorgeous." Carly hiccupped gently and stared after Lily's backside, retreating through the living room to the kitchen. "Pity I'm straight."

"And married."

"Yeah. That too. But sometimes I wonder why I am." Her gaze fastened on Freya. "You're not straight, though. And you're not married. You could—"

Freya heaved an exasperated breath. "Meaning?"

"You could ask her out."

"We have *nothing* in common. Nothing except the wall between our flats."

"Yoga. You're both vegan. You both dress like rejects from the sixties. You both like women."

Freya ignored the insult to her dress sense. "And there you have it. Carly, you like men, right?"

Carly nodded, her head bouncing like an enthusiastic two-year-old's who'd been asked if she wanted lollies. "Oh yeah."

"Well, if a man came in here, and you had nothing in common with him except that you both like to fuck the opposite sex, would you ask him out?"

Carly gazed at the ceiling. "Depends what he looked like. But if I was in the market, was horny, and he was available, yeah, I would."

Freya snorted. "I'll ignore that. Your standards are not that low."

"Neither are yours," Carly retorted, "which is why you should look at what's under your nose before someone else snaps her up."

"Snaps who up?"

Lily moved lightly for a big woman. Her bare feet had made no sound on the wooden boards.

"Snaps you up." Carly smirked in Freya's direction. "I was just telling my lesbian friend here that she should snap up the gorgeous lesbian living next door."

"It doesn't quite work like that, Carly." Lily's smile flickered for a second before she composed her features.

"Exactly what I just told her." Freya's glance bounced off Lily's.

"Just because two women are both lesbian, doesn't mean they're going to hook up." Lily's glance had become a gaze. Freya was caught by the warmth and amusement dancing in her brown eyes.

"Were you listening?" Carly's surprise was comical. "That's exactly what Freya said."

"I didn't need to listen. I've heard it before. I bet Freya has too."

"Sorry." Carly didn't look it.

Lily gestured back into the flat. "I came to tell you that dinner is on the table."

When they were seated, Lily lit the large candles at either end of the table and pointed to each dish in turn. "Cauliflower with mustard and soy yogurt. Mushroom curry. Dahl. Brown rice with coriander, and poppadums. All vegan and gluten free of course and no added sugar." She glanced at Freya, still seemingly amused. "As you requested, ma'am."

The warmth in her eyes was catching, and Freya found herself smiling back. "It looks fantastic."

With Carly's more outspoken comments reined in, the conversation flowed. Freya was grateful for her presence at the table. Not that she would be here if Carly wasn't. Had the invitation been for her alone, she would have refused. As the conversation wound through books they had read—many in common—movies they had seen—not so much—and the pleasures of living in Grasstree Flat, Freya had to admit she was enjoying herself. Lily was relaxing company. She threw her head back to laugh wholeheartedly at something Carly had said, and Freya was captivated by the expanse of brown throat, smooth, soft-looking. Lily swallowed a mouthful of wine, and the movement as she swallowed, the ripple under the skin, made Freya want to press her lips to that place. What would Lily feel like? What would she be like in the throes of passion? Would she be as wholehearted about that as she was about everything else? She set her tumbler carefully to one side. She must have drunk too much wine if she was even thinking like that.

Carly held out her tumbler for more wine. "So, Lily, tell me what we can expect in your first sexuality workshop next week?"

Lily dribbled a small amount into Carly's glass. "Nothing confronting the first time. I don't want to make anyone nervous. The workshop isn't going to single anyone out or put anyone on the spot. We'll do some group exercises aimed at being comfortable in your own skin, learning to ask for what you want in bed."

Carly leant forwards, seemingly captivated by Lily's words. "I need that. Andy and I have been married for twelve years now. Sex was good at first. Now... Well, I think we're in a rut. And the more I ask him to... do stuff... he just refuses. So I don't go down on him in retaliation. And now we're both sniping at each other."

Freya sat back in her chair. The conversation was rapidly heading outside of her comfort zone. Sex belonged in the bedroom, not around the dinner table. She tilted her chair back and stared at the ceiling. The paintwork was fresh, a paler primrose than the walls. Lily must have painted the entire flat before she moved in. It had been dusty cream when Diane used the space.

"I'm hoping to learn ways of getting the communication back," Carly continued. "We can't go on the way we are. I worry about our marriage sometimes."

Freya sipped. It really was a very fine wine. And from what Lily had said, the winery was owned by women. By lesbians. She would have to look it up, maybe order some.

"I hope that's what you'll learn."

"What about you, Freya?" Carly propped her chin on her hand. "Are you going to come with me?"

"I've already said no." Somehow, it was harder to be snippy, to be abrupt, and well, rude, when she was sitting in Lily's flat, eating Lily's delicious meal.

"Why not?" Carly's tactless side simmered to the surface again.

Freya raised a shoulder. "You know why if you stop to think about it. Besides, I'm not in a relationship." She skewered a glance at the wine glass in Carly's hand. Should she be drinking if she was trying to get pregnant? She didn't know.

"Do you have to be in a relationship to come to your class?" Carly directed the question at Lily.

"No. Single people are equally as welcome. But if you don't want to attend"—her warm brown gaze nailed Freya with its intensity—"then no one is going to make you. It's not for everyone. Now, who's for dessert?"

The abrupt change of subject was sufficient distraction for Carly. "I have never turned down dessert," she proclaimed.

"Good. I hope you'll like this one."

"I'll help you with the plates." Freya rose too.

Lily's kitchen was cluttered with dirty pots and pans, and knives and chopping boards were spread over the bench. Lily moved to the fridge. "Is Carly okay?" Her voice was muffled by the fridge. "I don't know her well at all, but she seems unhappy about something. I don't mean to pry and I don't want you to break a confidence, but I wondered if there was anything I could do to help."

Head tilted on one side, Freya regarded Lily's back. "She's having a bit of a rough patch in her marriage. She seldom drinks much—she's a two-pot screamer—so I think the wine has gone to her head."

"She's only had a couple of glasses."

"That's one more than she usually has. I don't think she's in a good headspace at the moment. I'll walk home with her, see if she wants to talk."

"That's good of you." Lily turned, a dense-looking cake in her hand. She went over to the stove and turned on the gas. "Here, stir this, will you?"

With her back to Lily, Freya found talking was easier. Easier to focus on the words, on the warmth in Lily's voice, if she wasn't looking at her nemesis. "Carly's not normally this much of a lush. She's usually the one drinking mineral water." She concentrated on stirring the contents of the pot—some sort of lemon syrup.

"On the sign-up form for the sexuality class, I asked participants to write what they hoped to get out of the class. Carly wrote she hoped to improve her marriage. I don't think I'm breaking a confidence telling you that."

Freya nodded. "Andy's not the worst. Somewhat uncaring, takes her a bit for granted. Like most men."

Lily was silent for a moment. "And some women." The rawness in her voice was unexpected.

Freya kept stirring. The timbre of Lily's voice reverberated in her head. It had been pained, as if Lily had personal experience with a relationship that wasn't that great. She probably had. She was maybe early thirties. Few people reached that age unscathed. And, Freya remembered with a jolt, Lily's wife had left her for a winemaker in Western Australia. A maker of very fine wines too, not that that had any bearing on Lily's pain.

She'd stopped stirring whilst she'd thought, and she moved the spoon around again to free up the sugar sticking to the bottom of the pan. "Did your wife…?" It was hard to continue. Not because she didn't have the empathy for conversations like this, not because she didn't want to reach out to someone. No, she did that often in her life and her work. It was because that person was Lily. Lily, whom she'd been practically feuding with. Freya hesitated and the spoon moved faster. She could stop the conversation right there. She could ask Lily some inane question about the syrup she was stirring. She could make a snarky comment about there obviously being a lot of sugar in the syrup when she'd expressly said she didn't eat much sugar. That would be on par with how she'd treated Lily so far. She opened her mouth, but the words died unsaid. That would be callous.

She cleared her throat. "Did your wife take you for granted?" She turned around abruptly enough that drips of syrup fell from the wooden spoon to splatter the stovetop.

Lily's mouth turned down in a rueful way. "No. I wish that had been the case. I was the one who took her for granted.

And look what happened. She left me. Left me for someone so very like me in many ways, but so much better in one: she had time for Inga. She cared for her, appreciated her. Listened to her. Really listened, not the half-arsed 'yes, honey' that many people do."

Lily turned back to the counter, leaving Freya with the impression of deep dark eyes and an aura of sadness.

"I've made pistachio lemon cake." Lily pushed the plate towards Freya. "Wheat-free and vegan. I know you said you don't eat much sugar, so if you would prefer to leave off that lemon syrup you're stirring, I can cut some slices for you before I pour it over the rest."

"Thank you. That's very thoughtful." Freya gave the syrup a final twirl with the spoon. "But I'd enjoy this, I think *some* sugar every so often doesn't hurt."

Lily's smile reached her eyes, turned them a deeper, warmer shade of brown, like the sheen of tree bark after rain. "I'm glad." Their gazes met, clung for a moment, and Lily was the first to break away. "Carly will think we've forgotten her."

Chapter 8

FAR FROM MISSING THEM, CARLY had moved to the couch and sprawled with her head against the back, sound asleep. Tiny whiffling snores rumbled from her open mouth.

"Should we let her sleep?" Lily set the plates on the table.

"I think she'd be more upset if she missed dessert." Freya sat next to Carly and put a gentle hand on her knee. "Carly, wake up. Sugar time."

Carly muttered something and turned around, bringing her feet onto the couch and resting her head on Freya's lap.

Freya huffed a sigh and put a hand on Carly's shoulder. "Carly, there's dessert." She needed Carly awake. She didn't have to be a fully functioning part of the conversation, but she wanted her for protection. Protection against the intimacy and unexpected rapport forged with Lily in the kitchen. She'd been a heartbeat away from asking Lily more about her wife. *Wife.* She didn't want to think too deeply on that one.

And if she learnt more about Inga, the next step would be some sharing of her own background. Her past relationships. Relationship, she amended. Singular. With Sarah. For although she'd had several relationships in her life, only one mattered. Only one still had the potential to rip her heart into tatters.

"Wassup?" Carly sat up slowly, blinking. She looked around at the other two. "Dessert? Did someone say dessert? Please tell me you haven't eaten it all."

"Far from it." Freya's comment came out harsher than she intended. "Plenty here for you, Sleeping Beauty."

Carly swung her feet to the floor and returned to the table. Lily cut a large slice of cake for her. "Dig in." She cut a second, equally large slice and gestured to Freya. "Here's yours."

There was silence as they ate, but it was a comfortable one.

"That cake was amazing." Carly, who'd woken up considerably, pushed her empty plate away with a sigh. She set her elbows on the table. "So what did I miss?"

Lily grinned at Freya. "Nothing much. We were discussing cake, and Freya said she'd walk home with you."

"Was I that obnoxious?" Carly's lips twisted ruefully. "Sorry. I'm okay now. I'll get home by myself."

"It's a fine night for a stroll, though." Lily poured water and sipped. "I love walking on nights like this. Stars. Few streetlights. Cicadas and frogs on a warm evening. Makes me wish I had a dog."

Carly glanced sideways at Freya. "Wonder how Dorcas would take living next door to a dog?"

"I'm not seriously thinking of it." Lily smiled in Freya's direction. "Dorcas is safe."

Freya's fingers tightened on her water glass. She took a deep breath. There had been another woman whose concern for Dorcas's wellbeing had prevented her getting a dog. She swallowed hard, aware Carly was staring at her, a small frown creasing her forehead.

"That's what Sarah used to say." The words welled up from within. Somewhere deep. Somewhere she normally kept locked up tight, buried under a welter of denial, an unwillingness to let them loose. Dimly, she saw Lily's questioning face and Carly's worried one. Carly knew well what Freya was thinking right now, as after all, Carly had been there when Sarah faded away. Carly had been there at the hospice when Sarah breathed her last. Not in the room with Sarah, but out in the waiting area. Deep in the middle of the night, Carly had come to be with Freya leaving Andy snoring at home. Carly had waited whilst Sarah slipped away so that she could hold Freya, offer wordless comfort, offer reassurance that although the world had ended, although Sarah was gone, Freya was not alone. She was still loved.

"Sarah wanted a dog." The words were rusty. "But she never got one because of Dorcas. She said Dorcas was there first and it wouldn't be fair to expect her to coexist with a dog. That was seven years ago, she said that. Four years before she… before she…"

Carly stretched out a hand and grasped Freya's. Her fingers hung limp in Carly's grasp, as if she would never feel them alive again, feel the tingles of joy, tingles of life.

"You can say it." Lily's fingers stroked the back of Freya's other hand where it rested on the glass. With gentle fingers, she removed the tumbler and placed her hand over Freya's, turning it around so their fingers were linked.

Freya was silent. Warmth moved into her from the clasp of hands. Energy. Her best friend, Carly. And Lily.

She took a deep breath. She could talk about Sarah. She could. Carly had loved her as a friend, Carly missed her still. And Lily… She was a lesbian. She would understand.

"What happened to Sarah?" Lily's voice was soft and the fingers that tightened over her own were comforting.

"Breast cancer. She was only thirty-seven, so she hadn't had a mammogram, was too young for the screening program. No family history. When she found the lump, it had already spread." Dimly, she thought this must be what it must feel like to be under hypnosis. The calm, silent room, the dim lighting, the gentle touch on her skin. The soothing voice. The urge to tell all.

"Tell me something about her. What was she like?"

"She loved to walk in the bush, took joy at being outside in the sunshine. Every day, she'd walk along the river by herself and come home and tell me about the black snake that crossed her path, a fish that jumped in the water, how the wildflowers had unfurled. Tiny flowers in the bush. She saw them all. She loved to prepare food and then watch people enjoy it." Freya clasped her water glass with both hands, needing the absence of her friends' touch to continue. "She said water was the finest and most beautiful drink of all. She appreciated it as others did a fine wine."

Carly propped her chin on her hand. "She loved reading. If she recommended a book to me, I'd go and buy it, as I knew I'd love it."

"She had great literary taste." Freya's mouth twisted. "Very highbrow at times, but she was no snob. If a genre romance was a great read, she'd recommend that too."

"Was she also involved in the shop?" Lily rose and went over to a dresser in the corner and collected some glasses and a dark bottle. She returned to the table and set down the bottle. A muscat from Victoria. "Would you like some?" She quirked an eyebrow at Freya. "Or I have tea if you prefer."

"I'll have some, please." The thought of the fortified wine was appealing.

"Carly?"

"I'll stick with water, thanks."

Lily poured two small glasses of muscat and topped up Carly's water glass.

"The shop was Sarah's before it was mine," Freya continued. "It's how we got together. I was teaching yoga and meditation in Mackay and running weekly classes in some of the smaller towns around, including Grasstree Flat. That's how I met Sarah—she came to one of my classes. Yoga became coffee, became a friendship. Then a date. Six months later, I moved to Grasstree Flat to be with her and we worked together."

Lily's dark gaze was fixed on Freya's face. She had kind eyes, non-judgmental. She invited confidences. She must hold all sorts of secrets, told to her by friends and strangers. Freya sipped her muscat. One part of her mind whispered that she would regret this in the morning. Sharing memories was as intimate—more intimate—than sharing bodies. Bodies were always on display; they could never be truly hidden. Memories, in particular the memory of a person, those were internalised. Nobody could know a memory, unless you chose to share it with them.

But still the words tumbled out into the room, into the flicker of candlelight, and the soft sounds of jazz still playing in the background. Freya's words slipped into the spaces between the susurration of breath, took form and flight in the high-ceilinged room.

"Sarah was my soulmate." Her breathing was shallow, from the upper part of her lungs. Her head spun from more than the alcohol.

Carly reached out again and grasped Freya's hand. "I know, darling. You two were everything I aspired for in a relationship. You shared your lives, your work, your interests. And love. You had so much love."

Freya squeezed Carly's hand and released it. "We'd talked of having a child. Sarah wanted to parent, to see how she could influence a small person to be what they would be in the world. She wanted to carry a child. I was happy to go along with that. Sarah would have been an incredible mother. She was the nurturing kind. But we never got beyond the talking stage."

"Maybe in your future you can consider it." Lily's fingers passed lightly over Freya's forearm and then retreated, as if she didn't want to push the connection.

"Maybe. It was always more Sarah's dream than mine."

The touch of light fingers again, in sympathy or understanding, Freya didn't know which. She could fall into this. This caring and sharing, and before she knew it, her life would be out in the open, her memories no longer hers. Thoughts and images of Sarah, the moving map of Sarah that lived in her head.

A curl of anxiety unfurled in her chest, crushing the mellow buzz of alcohol. She couldn't allow Sarah's memory to be diluted in that way. Sarah was still a part of her; as long as she held the memories close to her heart, Sarah would never be truly gone. As long as those memories were hers alone.

She straightened in her chair, centred herself, drew in a deep breath, held it, exhaled through her mouth. As she drew breath again, she inhaled the memories of Sarah and pushed them back down inside her where they belonged.

Freya tried to summon the steely resolve needed to put her boundaries back in place. Piece by piece, she shored up the wall around herself, knit together the boundary again. But the chinks from the evening remained. Carly and Lily, crumbling her defences slowly, like moss clings to stone.

"I should go," Freya said. "I have an early class in the morning. My prenatal ladies." She placed her hands flat on the table and stood. "Carly, would you like me to walk home with you?"

Carly blinked, as if mentally wool-gathering. "Uh, no, it's fine. I'm good." She stood and adopted tree pose. "See? Steady as rock." The pose wavered and she put a toe to the floor for balance. "A wobbly rock maybe, but still a rock."

Lily's face was washed clean of all expression. But if she understood Freya's reasons for running, she didn't call her on it.

"I can walk home with you if you want, Carly. That way Freya can prepare for her class."

A flicker of resentment spluttered: Lily was now usurping her friend. But even as the lick of anger died, Freya acknowledged that was unfair. Lily was only acting out of concern for Carly. Freya nodded at Lily, an echo of her earlier reserve seeping back. "Sure, if you don't mind."

"Why don't you both come?" Carly held out a hand to each of them. "It's not far. Twenty minutes will have you both back home again. And it's a lovely night. Come on." She steamrollered them towards the door, as if she were four, not thirty-four. She glanced back at the table, with the dirty plates and crumpled napkins. "Unless you want a hand cleaning up?"

Lily disengaged her hand from Carly's. "No, don't worry about it. Let's go, then."

Freya preceded the others down the stairs and out into the street. Carly was right; it was a gorgeous night. Still and clear, with a blaze of stars overhead. She turned to Lily. "There's no need for you to come. She hesitated, wondering whether to kiss her on the cheek. It implied a friendship, an intimacy she wasn't sure they shared, despite their earlier accord. She settled for a squeeze of the hand. "Thank you for a wonderful evening and a lovely dinner. I must get the recipe for that lemon pistachio cake from you."

"You're very welcome." Lily's eyes were huge in the silvery moonlight. It washed the quiet street with its cool glow. "I'm glad you were able to come." She turned to Carly. "Thank you for coming. I'll see you soon." She kissed Carly on the cheek.

"Hey, not so fast with the goodbyes." Carly manoeuvred herself between them. "You're both coming for the walk. Walk off that wine." She linked an arm through both of theirs and started purposefully down the street.

Carly's tight grip on her arm left Freya little choice. On nights like this in the past, she and Sarah had meandered arm-in-arm along the river path, a very different experience to Carly's forced route-march. She looked across to see what Lily made of this, but Lily looked comfortable, bustling along far faster than Freya would have expected.

They didn't talk in the ten minutes it took to reach Carly's modest weatherboard cottage. The house was dark. Andy must have gone to bed—or was still in the pub.

"Got your key?" Lily asked Carly.

"Don't need it. Who locks their house around here? Goodnight, and thank you both for walking me home." Carly pressed a kiss to Freya's cheek and then one to Lily's. She slid out of the three-way clasp, turned, and linked Freya's arm through Lily's.

"Safe home, girls. See you soon." She was gone, leaving Freya standing in the dark street, far too close to Lily.

"I'm not sure she needed the escort home." Amusement bubbled in Lily's voice, but she didn't disengage her arm.

"You're probably right. But I'm glad we gave her the opportunity to talk anyway." Freya's arm felt hot where it pressed against the soft pad of Lily's forearm. She slid her arm away and put a pace of distance between them.

"It's a beautiful night for a walk." Lily turned for home at a much easier pace than the one they'd taken to get there.

Freya pressed her reluctant legs into service and caught up. She was glad Lily didn't attempt conversation. She wasn't sure what she would say to her, not now, not after the unexpected intimacy of dinner, not after what was surely Carly's blatant attempt to throw them together. She said nothing and simply walked beside Lily through the quiet streets of Grasstree Flat.

Back at the shops, Freya turned to her. "Thank you for dinner. I enjoyed it." It was true. The words were polite, what you would say to anyone who had cooked you a meal, but the evening had been pleasant and filled with unexpected accord. Freya looked at Lily's smooth cheek; what would it feel like against her lips? She wondered, too, what would happen if she kissed it. Would Lily turn into the kiss? Try to make it something more? After all, Lily was a physical creature, given to sensual pleasures.

But then Lily smiled, and with a soft "I'm glad you enjoyed the evening. I did too. Goodnight," she slipped inside, leaving Freya staring at the black painted door.

Chapter 9

PINE NUTS. LILY RUMMAGED TO the back of the cupboard
in the vain hope she might find a bag she'd forgotten about. It
was hardly an unusual item, but Grasstree Flat's small general
store had none on the shelves. The organic produce store on the
main street stocked them in the big serve-yourself bins, but, as
with most shops in rural Australia, that store closed at noon on
Saturdays, and it was now three in the afternoon.

Lily glared at her cake ingredients lined up on the counter,
at the dates soaking in black tea, at the almond meal already
mixed with eggs. There was no substitute for pine nuts in her
recipe.

In Sydney, she could go out day or night and find a Middle
Eastern store or a chain supermarket and purchase pine nuts.
She blew out a breath. It served her right for not planning her
weekend baking frenzy better. A polenta flan cooled on the
counter. Almond pinwheels were in the oven. But unless she
found some pine nuts quick smart, her date-and-rosemary cake
would remain unbaked.

There wasn't a particular reason why she was baking. On
a day when unseasonal rain lashed the hills, she'd prowled

restlessly around her flat, unable to settle to do the accounts, or even to read a steamy novel. Due to the weather, she'd cancelled her plans with a woman who worked in one of Grasstree Flat's many op shops. Janie was funny and sparky, energetic and outgoing, and Lily had been looking forwards to their planned bushwalk in the national park. A walk that had the potential to be a little bit more. Janie's interest in Lily was obvious: her come-on unmistakable. She had also signed up for Lily's class, and had said with a saucy grin that she looked forwards to putting the knowledge into action.

Lily still wasn't entirely sure why, when she'd cancelled she hadn't suggested that Janie hang out at her place. An invitation which would have been as obvious as "come up for coffee." Had Janie come around, Lily was sure they would have seen out the cool, wet day from the warmth of her bed. Maybe watched the rain falling in a steady curtain as they lay entwined and naked on her pale green sheets. Maybe they would have eaten almond pinwheels in bed, getting nutty crumbs all over those same green sheets and all over each other. Maybe Lily would have tasted those same crumbs from Janie's skin, seeking them out with her tongue.

She hadn't had a woman in her bed for a while. Five months almost exactly. After Inga had left, she'd had a one-night stand with a woman she'd met at Mardi Gras. There had also been a couple of dates—and kisses—with a sweet and shy librarian. And then she'd moved to Grasstree Flat and there had been nothing except her own fingers and a variety of sex toys. Janie would have been an opportunity for fun, hot, sweet sex.

Except she'd made an excuse, and instead of spending the day with Janie, she was spending it cooking.

She blew strands of hair from her forehead. Where would she get pine nuts in Grasstree Flat on a Saturday afternoon? Carly could barely cook so much as an omelette, and she couldn't ask Janie now. Her gaze glanced off the party wall between her flat and Freya's. Freya probably had pine nuts sealed in a glass jar, neatly labelled and filed in her pantry between oatmeal and quinoa. Since dinner a week ago, she'd only seen Freya at yoga or heard her moving around on the other side of the thin wall. She hadn't bumped into her prickly neighbour.

Lily didn't want to think too hard why that was not a good thing.

Leaving the mess on the counter, she went down to the porch she shared with Freya and rang the bell. Instead of the usual buzz, there was silence. The bell must have broken. She rapped on the glass with as much force as she could muster, a smart rat-a-tat-tat. Again, nothing. Not for the first time, she wished she had Freya's phone number. It was what neighbours did; exchange numbers. What if there was a fire, or Dorcas strayed, or Freya wanted Lily to water her herbs in the backyard? She was just about to knock again when she heard the tread of feet moving towards the door. It swung open, and Freya stood there. She'd been obviously caught unawares; her face was relaxed and soft, a half smile curved her lips. Every other time Lily had seen her, her mouth had had a hard, uncompromising set to it. Except for the last time, over dinner, talking about her partner. Sarah. Then, Freya had worn an aura of sadness, an air of life passing her by. Then she had been human.

"Hi." Freya swiftly hid her look of surprise. "Is something the matter?"

Lily smiled. "I'm hoping you can help me. I'm baking and I'm right out of pine nuts. I know I've got Buckley's chance of finding any in Grasstree Flat at this time on the weekend, but I thought you might have some you could lend me."

Freya's answering smile was brief, but it was there. "I think so. Come in and I'll look."

Lily followed her ramrod back up the stairs, her grey-streaked hair swinging lightly. She'd never seen it loose before. Freya wore her hair rigidly controlled for yoga, and the rest of the time a bandana contained it. Now, unbound, it was thick, with a slight wave to it that brushed her shoulder blades.

She followed Freya to the neat kitchen. The only thing out of place was a box of Assam tea and a dirty mug on the counter. Freya opened one of the overhead cupboards and rummaged, setting aside bags of walnuts, almonds, buckwheat, and besan flour before pulling out a small bag of pine nuts.

"Will this be enough?"

"Thank you, yes. I only need about fifty grams. This will be plenty." Lily rested her hip against the bench, suddenly reluctant to take the pine nuts and leave. "I'm baking an almond, date, and rosemary cake. It's wheat-, sugar-, and dairy-free and utterly delicious. I'll bring you a slice."

"Sounds good. You're obviously a proficient baker. The cake you made at dinner was fabulous."

"Too proficient." Lily slapped her backside and grinned. "If I baked less, there might be less of this."

Freya's gaze snapped to Lily's butt, as though she was enjoying what she was seeing. Lily let her fingers remain there, smoothing a circle over her ample cheek with her palm.

Freya's gaze followed the movement. Seemingly with an effort, she cleared her throat. "You look fine to me."

"Oh?" Lily cocked a brow. "You're in the minority, then. Many people find big does not equate to beautiful. Or they assume I'm big because I eat junk or am welded to my couch."

"One of the myths of modern society." Freya's gaze travelled up Lily's body, back to her face, and Lily was caught in the piercing silver of her eyes. "I would put you at healthier than most people."

She inclined her head in acknowledgment. "Thanks. Now if I could just find a girlfriend who thought as you did, life would be sweet."

Why had she said that? Where was her verbal Delete key when she needed it? Now Freya would think it was a come-on, a hint as broad and wide as the Pioneer River, as unsubtle as a road map to her bed. Freya had made it perfectly obvious she was not in the market for a girlfriend. Indeed, to Lily's untrained eye, she still seemed to be grieving her dead partner. She cast around for a subject change. "How do you find that brand of Assam tea? I'm not too fond of the one I've been getting, but it's all they stock in the store here." Great. She'd just dug herself a deeper hole. Now Freya would think she was angling for an invitation for—

"I get it in Mackay. Would you like a cup?"

"Thanks, but I won't hold you up. Maybe I could take a bag with me to try?"

"It's no trouble. I was about to have another one anyway. You'll be doing me a favour. If you stay for a cup, you'll be keeping me from my accounts, and that's a good thing."

"In that case, I'd love one."

Freya flicked the switch on the kettle and found another mug. They waited for the kettle to boil in silence, but it wasn't an awkward one. It was the sort of accord between people who, whilst they may not be friends, had moved beyond the inane chatter that strangers employ to fill silences.

When Freya had made the tea, Lily followed her out to the balcony. The afternoon was warm, the heat making the hills on the far side of the flat shimmer with the blue haze of eucalyptus. Dorcas appeared, made a beeline for Lily, and stepped onto her lap with delicate paws. Once she'd curled into a ball, her purrs rumbled like Queensland Rail.

"Have you heard from Carly since our dinner?" Lily stroked along Dorcas's spine with one finger, smiling at how the cat undulated under her touch.

"She called the next day to apologise for falling asleep." Freya took a sip of tea and her gaze flicked sideways to Lily. "And to hope I hadn't taken offence at being thrown together with you."

Lily's breath caught in her throat. Of all the things she thought Freya would say, she never thought she would even acknowledge Carly's matchmaking. "What did you say?"

"I made her sweat." Amusement rippled through Freya's voice. "I said she knew my thoughts on dating and relationships very well, and I would appreciate it if she honoured them."

The heavy weight of disappointment that settled in Lily's belly took her by surprise. Freya had made her lack of physical need very clear—so why did her comment feel so personal?

"I let her off the hook. I said it was no big deal." Lightness and humour hummed in Freya's voice. "But I told her again that my path was a spiritual one."

"And mine is grounded in physicality. My body, my skin. I'm surprised Carly even thought we would be interested in each other in that way."

Freya shrugged. "Just because she doesn't know many lesbians, she assumes there are not many around. In fact, this little town has more than the 10 percent average, I'm sure of it."

"I've met a few, and there's plenty of rainbow flags around town. I should ask you to introduce me around."

"From what I've already heard, you're finding your way just fine by yourself."

Lily stored that information away. Janie, she presumed. It made sense. A small town, a smaller lesbian community. To answer seemed to be asking for trouble, leading the conversation in a direction she wasn't sure she wanted it to go.

"How long have you had Dorcas?" she asked instead.

"Seven years. She was a wee ball of fluff abandoned in a back alley in Mackay. Sarah found her just after we got together. Someone had put her in a garbage bag and tied it up tightly. It was a stinking hot day, and Sarah heard her faint cries as she walked past. She got her out and took her home. At first, we weren't sure she would make it."

Lily petted the cat's soft fur. "She's lucky."

"We were lucky too. She's been a loving companion."

The tea was cooling. Lily swallowed a couple of mouthfuls. "I better go. I left a half-prepared cake on the bench. I should get back and finish it." She nudged Dorcas gently until the cat took the hint and unwound herself from Lily's lap. "Thank you for the tea, and the pine nuts."

"I can get you some of that tea the next time I'm in Mackay, if you'd like."

"I would. Thank you."

Then there seemed to be nothing to say. Lily led the way downstairs and out through Freya's shop to the porch. The afternoon shade cast Freya into shadows as she stood in the doorway.

Lily turned towards her. The muted colour of Freya's clothes blended into the darkness of the shop, turning her into a mysterious thing of shade and shadow. Then she moved forwards, out to the footpath, and her wiry curls caught the light, turning it into a spun cage of sunshine.

Freya touched the drooping leaf of one of her plants. "I'll have to water these."

The line of her arm had an elegance Lily hadn't associated with her down-to-earth neighbour. Her gaze traced the lean shape down to where Freya's long fingers with their short, blunt nails, traced the leaf with care.

Her words came with an effort. "Thanks for the tea. I'll bring you some cake in the morning."

The afternoon had lost some of its allure. Lily added the pine nuts to the cake and baked it to perfection, then made pasta for dinner. But the meal wasn't as enjoyable when eaten alone, and the glass of wine she allowed herself was uninteresting in her mouth. She tipped it out and poured a glass of water instead. Sarah had likened water to fine wine. If she was as discerning in her choice of partner as she was with water, then Freya and she must have been good together.

She took the water out onto the balcony and propped her feet on the low table as she stared down the street. The water tasted fresh and cool. Lily rolled it around in her mouth, tasting it as if it were wine. Is this how Sarah had done it, she wondered? Sipping and enjoying?

Freya had said she and Sarah were together for seven years. Three years longer than Lily and Inga had been partners. Lily rested her head on the back of the couch. Inga sprung into her mind, her slim body with the deepest, darkest brown eyes. Their years together rolled through Lily's head in a flickering cinematic parade of moments: the day they'd met, sharing a table at a local coffee shop. The first kiss. Their first time in bed, and that slow, soft exploration of lovemaking. They hadn't left the bed all day, except to pee and to raid the fridge for snacks and wine. They had moved in together three weeks later, after finding a flat together in a subdivided Victorian terrace house in inner Sydney. Inga grew herbs on the windowsill. Lily mastered the cranky old oven and started baking. Their lives had stitched together so easily that, looking back, Lily remembered only the times of joy and contentment.

And now, here she was by herself in a small town light years from Sydney. She sipped her water slowly, and the bitter taste of aloneness clung to the back of her throat.

She missed it. Not just Inga, who would forever hold a piece of her heart, but the closeness that comes with loving someone and being loved in return.

Her mouth twisted wryly. If many of the women who knew her in Grasstree Flat were privy to her thoughts, they'd probably think she'd sold out to suburbia. But whilst she loved the sexual freedom and playfulness being single offered, if the right woman came along, if she fell in love again, if the woman loved her…

Lily set her water on the table. Was there a woman for her, here in Grasstree Flat? There was Janie, and she knew of other lesbians here.

And there was Freya.

Chapter 10

FREYA NODDED TO LILY AS she took what was now her usual spot near the back. Lily laid out her mat, said a few words to the woman next to her, and stood straight and tall, waiting for the yoga class to begin. This time, she wore a cherry-red top with purple leggings, which were so bright that even when Freya looked away, she saw the flash of colour on the edge of her vision.

Lily's earlier awkwardness was gone as she moved through the poses. She had settled back into what was obviously a long-time activity. Freya had hoped to catch her at the end of the class to thank her for the cake that had been left in a container on her doorstep the morning after Lily had borrowed the pine nuts. The cake had been incredible; a creamy blend of unusual flavours that melded seamlessly together. The morning after that, there had been a bag of pine nuts on the step. Why Lily hadn't rung the bell, Freya didn't know, but she shrugged it off.

But when Lily slipped through the door back to her shop with a smile at the end of class, Freya realised the missed opportunity to compliment her on the cake.

Carly waited for her. "Well? Are you coming?"

Freya lifted an eyebrow. "To what? Coffee?"

"No. Lily's class. It's the first one this afternoon. She's closing an hour early today. Exploring Your Feminine Sensuality. C'mon, Frey. Come with me."

"I've already said no." She softened her words with a smile. "It's not my thing."

"Lily attends your class. You could support her; she's new in town."

"It's not a tit-for-tat thing. And from what I've heard, there will be a few people there. She doesn't need me. And I'd have to close early too."

"Lily might not need you, but I do." Carly's voice was a pathetic whine. "Maybe I'm too nervous to go alone."

"Maybe you're not. You're the one banging on about this class."

"Okay, so I'm not nervous. I'm looking forwards to it. But it would be good if you were there." A sly peep from under her eyelashes. "You might learn something."

"I'm sure I would. Whether I need that knowledge is another thing entirely."

Carly heaved a sigh. "Final answer?"

"No."

"I'll tell you what it's like."

"If you must."

Carly's expression sobered. "Okay. I won't go on about it. Now, do you have time for coffee?"

"Coffee and breakfast. Of course." She squeezed Carly's hand. "Lead on, Mata Hari."

"Ohhhhhhh. Ohhhhhhhhhh! Oh, yes, yes, yes!" The jubilant cries ended on a high keening note. Freya closed her eyes momentarily and clenched the pen in her hand. For once, she was actually grateful there were no customers in her shop to overhear the sounds coming through the thin walls from the studio. The *yoga* studio. Or the writing workshop. But whatever it was, it was for quiet, inward pursuits. Not this loud expression of faked sexual pleasure.

Mercifully, the woman on the far side of the wall fell silent. Now Freya heard the rise and fall of Lily's tones, then the ripple of laughter from the participants. Her teeth ached from gritting them, and her body was rigid from holding in the need to storm into the yoga studio and shout at everyone to be quiet. That pleasure was private, even the artificial noises of imaginary pleasure Lily seemed to be teaching her class. She didn't want to hear it. She didn't *need* to hear it.

She relaxed her posture, reached for her water bottle and took a deep drink, and returned to her orders.

"I want it all. I want it now." The low chant pulsed through the wall. The voices were rhythmic, increasing in volume. "I want it all. I want it now." The chant rose until it was a shout.

Freya threw down the pen. The noise was intrusive, impossible to block out. She rose and moved to the front of the shop and started rearranging a display of silver earrings. Here was blessed silence. But then a low moan rose in pitch like that of a dying whale. Even here, she couldn't escape. She returned to the rear of the shop and turned on her music streaming, picking a channel that was louder and more vibrant than the soothing tunes she normally chose.

But she could still hear the chanting when it resumed, an undercurrent of annoyance even over the Aussie rock coming from her speakers. She glanced at her watch. It would be time to close in fifteen minutes. With luck, there would be no customers in the meantime. But this couldn't be permitted; Lily's class was disrupting her business. Freya turned up the volume on the streaming service. It was now so loud, she didn't hear the Indian chimes that signalled a customer had entered the shop, and it was only the flash of movement near the front that caught her eye. Freya gritted her teeth. It was Brigid, one of her most irritating—and demanding—customers.

"Hello, what can I help you with today?"

Brigid's mouth was turned down in a moue of distaste. "Some of the sage cleansing sticks I got last time."

Freya moved the single step necessary to get the sage from the shelf.

"And the rosemary-and-mint soap."

Another single step in the other direction.

"I hope this music isn't always going to be playing. I always thought this was a tasteful, refined shop. Not like the monstrosity next door."

Freya smiled. "I'm simply trying out a new channel. I'm not too fond of it, either." Even though she was tempted to complain about Lily's shop, this whinging old biddy was not to be encouraged.

"Good. It doesn't entice me to stay and browse. Now that lovely Norah Jones... She knows how to carry a tune."

Freya's mouth made the appropriate polite smile as she carried Brigid's purchases over to the counter.

A low moan came from the yoga room. It rose in pitch then fell silent. Brigid cocked her head. "Is someone else using your yoga room?"

"There's a class on."

"A new instructor. How nice. I shall have to take a look sometime. I never liked your yoga. Not enough consideration for older women and our bad joints."

Freya's lips tightened. The couple of times Brigid had come to a beginners' class, she had made no attempt to join in, merely stood there complaining loudly that she couldn't do the movements. Movements she wouldn't even attempt.

The streaming service stuttered in mid-song as the signal was interrupted. A quiet buzzing reached Freya's ears through the thin wall. It intensified for a moment, before shutting off. She drew a quick breath. She knew what a vibrator sounded like; she just hoped her customer didn't.

In the silence that followed, Lily's voice came clearly through the wall. "Choosing a vibrator is a very personal experience. Don't assume they are all the same. Intensity, speed, power, shape, all play a part. Even how it feels in your hand."

"Only your hand?" Another voice—Carly's.

The smile was evident in Lily's voice. "Not only in your hand. But adult shops can't let you return a vibrator once it has been used. I'm sure you can understand why. But we encourage you to fondle…"

Her voice trailed off as she must have moved further from the wall. Freya met Brigid's horrified gaze. "Really, Freya. I'm disappointed you let that sort of thing in your studio."

"It's a shared space with the shop next door."

"But Diane never used it."

Freya shrugged. "But she could have done. It's purely for use as a workshop space." A twist of her mind recognised the irony of defending Lily, however roundabout. But the woman in front of her, with her pinched lips and closed mind, reminded her of her teenage years, coming out in a middling-sized town in a strait-laced state in rural Australia. The disapproval she'd encountered then was echoed in the prim stance of the woman in front of her now. If she closed her eyes, she was sure Brigid would flash in front of them, her face transposed onto any of the disapproving teachers, parents, and other adults who'd tried to tell her that her sexuality—and by extension, herself—was wrong.

She smiled a genuine smile. "A Woman's Pleasure has a lot to offer all of us. They have a very colourful range of cushions and throws you might like." She neglected to mention that those same soft furnishings were emblazoned with stylistic depictions of female genitalia. "That will be seventeen dollars, please."

Brigid handed over her card without comment and Freya processed the sale. "Thank you. See you soon."

Brigid left without another word. Freya had the feeling she'd just lost a customer due to her defence of Lily's shop, and the class she hated. She sniffed. Her words had been spontaneous. That didn't mean she suddenly approved of the use of the space. Laughter rippled through the wall again overlaid with Lily's voice, although Freya couldn't hear what she said.

The streaming service hadn't restarted. Freya moved to the player and reset it back to the Aussie rock channel. There would be no more Norah Jones, not in her shop.

A couple more customers came in before closing time, but the activity on the other side of the wall was no more shocking than muted voices and shared laughter. But her jittery nerves had her glancing to the back wall often.

It was too bad. If this class was a weekly occurrence, she would be forever worried what her customers would overhear and if they would be offended. Brigid was a customer she didn't mind losing, but she couldn't treat them all that way. A shopkeeper needed to be a smiling, affable mind reader, delighted to see every customer, no matter how painful or annoying.

She moved to the shelf that held tisanes and flavoured teas, and ordered the boxes until they stood in neat soldier rows. She touched the yellow box of lemon balm and ginger tisane. It had been Sarah's favourite, and even though scarcely any of it sold, Freya still stocked it, still drank the occasional cup just to conjure her lover in the scent of lemon balm.

"What would you do, Sarah?" She directed the words at the display of tea, seeing in her mind Sarah's fingers plucking the box from the shelf as she'd often done when she ran out of it upstairs. "Would you have gone to the class?"

A niggle in the back of her mind told her that, yes, Sarah may well have attended. She'd been open to new things, new experiences. Even a naturist resort to feel the sun on her body. Even parachuting although she was scared of heights. Even a snake-handling course, although she disliked the feel of reptiles. But she'd given them a go. And a sexuality class? There was nothing Sarah would have disliked about that. At least, not in the first few years of their relationship.

It was just gone five thirty. She turned the sign to *Namaste. Return Again, Friend.* The sound of voices made her peer through the glass just as the group of women walked past. Carly was at one end, her curls bouncing as she bounded along in that puppyish way of hers. She was chatting with a woman Freya didn't recognise. The group moved slowly down the street. In their midst was Lily. Her dark hair was held back by a scarlet scarf, and she was laughing at something someone had said. As Freya watched, Lily placed a hand on the shoulder of the woman next to her and leant in closer to say something. The afternoon sunlight flashed off the silver rings in her ears. If the moment were frozen in a photograph, it would be captioned *Fun and Female Friendship: the Building Blocks of a Happy Life.*

"So are we going to the pub?" she heard.

"Oh yes!" That was Carly's voice. "There's a bucket of wine waiting for me, I'm sure of it."

Freya moved back from the glass. She didn't want anyone to turn and see her peeping out from her shop, a woman alone, not part of the group. Sidelined. But the image of them blurred in front of her eyes, Lily most of all. The effortless centre of attention.

She gathered herself, drawing in her strength, her female power, her aloneness. She didn't need the superficiality and physical excesses Lily represented. She was strong.

Freya quashed the tiny voice that whispered, what would it be like to have Lily touch her skin like that; what would it be like to feel her fingers clasp Freya's own? What if Lily looked at her, Freya, with those dark, expressive eyes, focused in on her so closely, so entirely. What would that be like?

She swallowed. Tendrils of something long buried stirred in her belly. A warmth, a spreading.

Desire.

Chapter 11

LILY PULLED A PAIR OF yoga pants and a T-shirt from the back of the wardrobe. She now attended yoga three times a week. Freya had begrudgingly given her the nod to come to an intermediate class, as well as the beginners' one. Each time she went, more moves came back to her. Muscle memory. It had been a while since her body had been so flexible.

The intermediate class had introduced her to a different group of people. Carly, of course, but she had been pleased to see a couple of women who also attended her sexuality workshop.

Yoga had been an unexpected pleasure in living in Grasstree Flat. She looked forwards to the hour out of her increasingly busy life, an hour when she focused on herself and her body, her wellbeing. She twisted her hair into a messy knot on the top of her head. That was something she always told her sexuality class. Make time for yourself, your body, your pleasure. Get to know yourself. Let your fingers do the walking.

She hadn't been doing that lately. The last time her fingers had drifted down between her legs in the peace of her own bed, she'd fallen asleep. She'd been so tired after the demands of her workshop and the constant tasks of a new business.

Maybe it was time to practice what she preached in class, and let herself experience more pleasure, sex without guilt or censure or shame. But then, as she told her students, it had to be right for *you*. Some people found their pleasure in one partner and a lifelong relationship. Others took a new partner often, yet others embraced a polyamorous lifestyle. There was no right way. No wrong way, as long as it was what all participants wanted and freely gave their consent.

The persistent woman from the bushwalking group pushed into her head. Janie. There'd been a spark between them. In Sydney, if she'd been free and available, she wouldn't have hesitated. Maybe it was finally time to explore some possibilities there.

Leaving her feet bare, Lily trotted down the worn timber stairs and through her shop to the studio. She smiled at her fellow classmates, and nodded to Freya, who stood tall and proud at the front, then Lily took her accustomed place at the rear.

"*Namaste*," Freya said. "Welcome. Today, in addition to focusing on core and balance, I want you all to adopt a pose that is comfortable for you. Close your eyes and focus on your breath, in through your nose, hold… and out through your mouth. Expand your awareness along the pathways in your body. Today, I want you to focus on those pathways you may have neglected. Let the energy flow along routes that are less used. Maybe it is an area of your mind, some thoughts you have ignored, a problem unsolved. Maybe it is a physical area, a muscle that is tight, a small ache or pain. Concentrate on that, let the energy flow."

Lily closed her eyes, breathed in and thought of her energy as a white light ready to be directed at her will. Where would it go? There was only one answer—the one she had been thinking of only that morning. Her pleasure, her sexual nature, was the most neglected part of her right now, despite how she was working to bring out that awareness in others.

Her visualisation settled deep in her belly, between her legs. The white light built to a low, pulsing energy that grew in intensity with each breath until she could barely stand it. For a few moments, she fought it—this yoga class was not the place—but the energy would not be denied. Her nipples tingled against the cotton fabric of her bra, and her pussy lips were engorged and heavy. Moisture pooled between her thighs. She tried to ignore it, focusing on her breath, trying to redirect her energy to other places. But her body would not be controlled; the only thing sucking the energy she was creating was her sex. Her mind and her sex.

With a small sigh, Lily gave herself up to the sensation, and her body swam in liquid heat, filled with a tingle and an *aliveness* that now threatened to consume her.

Dimly, she heard Freya's voice, bringing the class back from their inner journeys, back to the yoga studio. She didn't want to release this discovery, so she wound that energy tight, pushed it deep within, so she could call on it at another time.

She opened her eyes and found herself staring directly at Freya's intense silver gaze. Two rows of women sat between her and Freya, but the connection strung tight, a shining cord of energy linking the two of them.

But then Freya broke eye content and glanced around the room. "Mountain pose," she said.

To Lily's ears, Freya's voice was rougher than usual, a little hoarse. Had Freya felt that connection too, or was it all in her own head? She mentally shook herself. It was one thing to acknowledge the imbalance in her life that lack of sexual pleasure had brought; it was quite another to project that longing onto her neighbour, an abrasive seemingly asexual woman who had no desire to change that status.

Lily pushed the image of steely eyes and stern face from her mind and directed her thoughts to her own needs. Healing and change. Freya's words had sparked something, a seed of an idea that unfurled tiny tendrils in her mind as the class progressed.

Two things needed to happen: most immediately, she would explore herself with fingers and toys this evening. No TV, no books in bed, no time on the balcony with a glass of wine. Instead, she would rediscover the physicality of sexual pleasure. Her body hummed in acknowledgment and anticipation.

And the second thing? Maybe that would never happen as it involved Freya. It certainly wouldn't start today; indeed, it may never get off the ground. The approach would have to be as delicate and light as Dorcas when she balanced on the balcony railing. Lily would have to be careful, subtle, enticing rather than blunt. She would have to choose her words with care.

Lily moved into eagle pose. Her body stretched, her nerves tingled in anticipation. Not today, not tomorrow, but one day soon, Lily would propose to Freya that the two of them run a yoga and sexuality workshop together.

Over the next few days, Lily bided her time, but it was hard to get Freya alone, and with enough privacy and time to discuss her idea. She hung back after the intermediate yoga class, only to find that Carly, too, was waiting for Freya.

"We're going for breakfast at the Green House," Carly said. "Want to come?"

She had a million things to do—a new shipment of books from her favourite women's publisher had arrived, and her business activity statements were on the verge of being overdue at the tax office. But as she opened her mouth to accept anyway, and the tax office be damned, she caught the tiny tightening of Freya's lips. Maybe Freya wanted time alone with her friend, or maybe she just didn't want Lily along.

She declined with a regretful shake of her head, citing those damn tax office forms that wouldn't wait for breakfast.

"They do the most fantastic chia porridge," Carly tempted her.

"I know. I've had it. Maybe next time." And Lily walked away, to shower and change, and to move into her day.

Freya was true to her word, and the next morning, Lily found a packet of the Assam tea she had so enjoyed on her doorstep. She picked it up and turned it over in her hands. This would give her the excuse she needed to speak with Freya. After all, the tea was expensive; she must owe her money.

Without waiting to second-guess herself, she took the tea upstairs and grabbed her purse. It was only seven in the morning, but Freya was an early riser and was usually up long before this. She'd heard the light footfalls in the mornings, the sound of water in the shower, and sometimes the soft tones of a meditation chant wafting from the balcony in the dawn.

Freya answered her door after a couple of minutes, long enough that Lily had started to assume she was busy with her morning routine and didn't want to be disturbed.

"Hi." She held up her purse. "Thank you for the tea. What do I owe you?"

Freya's face was expressionless, her posture rigidly upright, at odds with her bare feet and the loose Indian pants she wore. "Don't worry about it. Enjoy the tea." The door started to close.

Lily pitched her voice louder against the closing door. "Actually, I wanted to talk to you about something anyway. A joint venture. Do you have a few minutes?"

Freya's bark of laughter wasn't encouraging. It had a sort of resigned coolness, as if anything Lily was to propose were doomed to failure and not worthy of consideration. "I suppose now is as good a time as any." She held the door wider. "Come in." She led the way to the balcony, which was still relatively cool in the morning shade.

Lily didn't wait for an invitation; she sat on the couch, made herself comfortable. A couple of pale-headed rosellas perched in the gum tree opposite, feeding on the flowers. Their blue-and-yellow plumage made bright patches in the grey-green of the leaves.

"I love those birds," she said. "You don't see them in Sydney."

Freya rested her butt against the railing. "You wanted to talk about something?"

"Yes, I do. But first, tell me what I owe you for the tea. If I don't pay you for it, I'll feel I can't ask you to get me some more, and it's gorgeous."

Freya shrugged. "If you insist. It's eight dollars."

Lily handed over a ten, which Freya pocketed. "I owe you two bucks."

Lily took a deep breath. "I've been thinking. Remember last week in yoga, you told us to focus on an area of ourselves that needed attention? Let the energy flow to that place, you said." Freya nodded, and Lily continued, "Well, there was an area in my life that's been somewhat neglected of late." Her pulse juddered at the thought of what she had to say next. "I've been neglecting my own sexual pleasure. I've been too busy, and then too tired to pursue that part of my life, which used to be such an important one. Indeed, I recognise the irony of teaching others how to expand their sexual pleasure when my own is withering." She snuck a glance at Freya's face. It wore a look of cool disinterest. Lily could have been talking about specials in the meat department of the local supermarket.

"When you talked about the energy flow, well, that was the area to which my energy went. Your yoga class revitalised my sexual energy."

Freya turned away and faced out over the street, as if the conversation were already over. "That's fine. I'm glad you took something out of the class."

"It made me think that you and I could run a class together. Yoga for sexual health and wellbeing."

Freya swung back to face her. "Yoga for *what*? I don't think so. I think our teaching methods and aims are completely incompatible."

"I respectfully disagree. We have many students in common. Our overarching aim in teaching has, at its core, the same goal: we want to give women joy and power in their lives. You do that with your yoga, I do that with my sexuality class. Your class the other day made me realise how very intertwined those two courses could be. A class focusing on meditation and yoga techniques to ground the physicality of sex."

"You're forgetting one thing." Freya's voice could have shredded paper. "I encourage people to rise above their baser desires to find happiness. You lower them to their animal instincts. Our classes could not be more different."

"You've never been to one of my classes."

"I don't need to. I heard it through the wall of my shop. Every. Damn. Word. I heard your casual approach to teaching, I heard the informality of your exchanges with students, and I certainly heard the sex toys you were demonstrating, as did my customer. I didn't want your shop next door to mine, I still don't, and I can't think of anything that would induce me to run a class with you."

Lily frowned. "You heard through the wall? I'm sorry, I didn't realise we were that loud."

"Single skin panelling. I hear your music, I hear you singing in the shower, talking on the phone. I hear most things."

"I seldom hear you."

"I'm extremely quiet by nature. You, obviously, are not. In *anything*."

The stress on the final word alerted Lily to what else Freya could have heard through the wall.

"I see. I'm sorry if that made you uncomfortable. That was the last thing on my mind."

"Obviously." The word was as dry as desert dust.

Lily fell silent. Any sort of response eluded her. She could hardly promise not to have more sessions with her favourite sex toys—especially since she had rediscovered her dormant sexual energy. And equally, a promise to keep quiet went against her nature. She liked to vocalise. The words, the grunts, the groans, the whispers and sighs, the occasional shriek of pleasure, well they were all part and parcel of sex. The only way she would be quiet was if someone smothered her with a pillow, and *that* wasn't going to happen.

"I can't promise to be quiet. It's just not my way. I'll move my bed away from the wall, though. That should make some difference." She smothered a giggle at the thought of Freya banging on the wall at Lily's most intense moment.

"I don't find this funny."

"No. I'm sorry it's difficult for you. I'll see if I can get some cloth wall-hangings. That should help muffle any noise." She cleared her throat. It must be nerves making her throat as dry as it was. The idea of the joint class had fired her enthusiasm in an entirely unexpected way. There must be some way she could persuade Freya to agree. "Please can I have a glass of water?"

Freya nodded and disappeared back into the flat. Lily sat back on the couch. Dorcas appeared from some cat hiding place and padded over the couch to curl up on Lily's lap.

"What do you reckon, Dorcas?" She stroked the cat along the spine, and Dorcas undulated under her hand and pushed her head against Lily's forearm. "I don't want to make your mum uncomfortable, but that's all I seem to do. I get that she doesn't want a physical relationship with anyone. That's her choice. No worries. But I can't live as she does." She fell silent, running her fingers lightly over the cat's fur. Animals were so calming; maybe she should get a cat herself. "You'd have a friend, Dorcas. Living right next door to you. Would you like that?" Although neighbours were not necessarily friends. She and Freya were proof of that.

Freya had taken a while to get the water. Lily closed her eyes and relaxed on the couch. Freya got under her skin in a way few people did. Her brusqueness, her insistence that life was best lived on some sort of esoteric, spiritual plane. If Freya ever changed her mind, if she decided to rejoin the sexual world, then Lily was sure she would find any number of willing partners in Grasstree Flat.

Freya returned and thrust a cool glass at Lily.

"Thanks." Lily drained it in long gulps and set it down beside her. "I don't mean to antagonise you, you know. All of this"—she waved her hand generally around, encompassing where they sat, the shops, even Grasstree Flat—"is just me, trying to live my life the way I've always wanted. And along the way, if I can help other people as well, that's great. I think that's probably how you see it too."

"I do. And I don't have a problem with your choices. It's when they impinge upon mine that the difficulties start. Your noise through the bedroom wall. Your classes in my workshop area—"

"Our workshop area."

"*Our* workshop area. I accept that, I have to, it's in the lease, but I can't accept you driving away my customers. Even you attending yoga... Well, now, it seems you want to usurp that as well with your latest scheme. Not only do you push your lifestyle in my face at every opportunity, now you want me to be a part of it." She glared at Dorcas, still curled on Lily's lap, as though the cat's defection was just another irritant. Like sand in her bathers, or a bindii in her sandal.

"I didn't expect you to agree just like that." Lily's words were subdued. She tried to summon her breezy exterior cheer, but it withered in the face of Freya's scorn. "I only hoped you might consider the idea."

"In your dreams." Freya bristled; even her hair crackled with antagonism, standing out around her sharp face in a wiry cloud.

Her dreams. They were another thing she couldn't control. Funny how Freya featured in those as well lately, but a softer Freya, a Freya with the same dry humour, but less prickly.

One who seemed to like Lily and wanted to share times with her. The previous night's dream had been about her and Freya having coffee together in Remy's café. Just coffee and cake. Nothing more, nothing less. Something simple that two friends who wanted to spend time with each other did on any given day of the week.

"I don't suppose you'd like to have coffee with me tomorrow morning after yoga?" The words popped out, an extension of the scenario in her head.

"Why? So you can proposition me with another lunatic idea?"

Proposition. The word caught Lily by surprise. *Proposition.* There were a few things she'd like to proposition Freya with. A sexuality and yoga class. Tick, been there, done that, strike one. Coffee. It appeared that was strike two. The third thing hovered there, dust and clouds, a nebulous thing she couldn't even articulate to herself. But it had been there in a dream, not last night, but one before then. A kiss. Herself kissing Freya with tenderness and a hint of passion. Her mouth twisted. Her unconscious mind was obviously on the same crazy plane as her conscious one. She wouldn't—couldn't—even articulate that one, as it would fly against everything Freya lived for.

"Just coffee. Maybe a cake. Treat ourselves." Her smile was a forced approximation of her usual one, but it was the best she could do. "Try and be friends. I thought we had a pleasant evening when you and Carly came to dinner."

Freya's nod was terse, but it was a nod. "I have breakfast with Carly after yoga. Come along too, if you want."

As invitations went, it was far from effusive, but it was a start.

"Sure. I'd like that."

Chapter 12

LILY WAS WAITING FOR FREYA after yoga the next morning. Her hair was tied back with what looked like a strip from a torn T-shirt, and her lilac yoga pants clashed horribly with her gold-and-brown tunic. The woman had more yoga clothes than were for sale in a medium-sized Queensland town. For a second, the image of another woman superimposed itself over Lily's garish figure. Sarah, dressed for yoga in a neat striped top and matching pants, but her long soft hair tied back with a similar-looking strip of cloth torn from a T-shirt. Freya had laughed and challenged Sarah on it.

"Can't you find a hairband?" she'd said.

Sarah had smiled, that genuine smile of hers, one that crinkled her eyes and etched a dimple in her cheek. "Sure," she'd said. "But I like this better. It reminds me of you." And Freya had looked closer and seen it came from one of her old T-shirts that she'd thrown in the rag bag only the day before, deeming it too worn and faded for day-to-day wear.

Freya shook herself, the image of Sarah receding like the tide. Lily stared at her quizzically, no doubt wondering why she'd frozen almost in mid-stride, her gaze locked on the middle distance. She forced an approximation of a smile and closed the remaining space.

Carly, too, was waiting, and the three of them walked the short distance to the Green House. Their usual table was free, and Carly dragged over a third chair. It was cramped with three of them, and Freya's arm rubbed against Lily's. Lily's flesh was warm. Freya inched closer to Carly.

"What can I get you three?" Remy stood in front of the table, pad in hand.

Lily studied the menu. "Please can I have the buckwheat pancakes with apple and cinnamon. And a cuban espresso. Thanks."

"Good choice." Remy turned to the others. "The usual? Brekky wrap, chia-and-pecan porridge, and coffee?"

"Yes, please," Carly said.

Freya closed the menu. "Actually, the buckwheat pancakes sound good. I'd like them, please, but with banana."

Carly goggled at her. "You *always* have the porridge."

"Sometimes it's good to change. I'm not totally set in my ways." She kept her eyes firmly fixed on Carly. This was about breakfast choices, it wasn't a deeper message. It didn't mean she was suddenly going to launch into a sex-and-yoga class with Lily.

Lily shifted again, and her upper arm brushed against Freya's. Freya tried to move her chair away, but her back was to the wall, and there was nowhere to go. She was silent, her awareness focused on the scant centimetres of space between herself and Lily.

Carly's chatter filled the awkward silence. "It's my birthday in two days' time. Thirty-five. Thirty-fucking-five. Why does that seem so old? That's halfway to forty."

"Technically, twenty is halfway to forty. And let's not forget that being forty is halfway to being dead." Freya took the opportunity to nudge Carly. The space between her and Lily grew another centimetre.

Carly's eyes widened. "I didn't mean that! Besides, you're the healthiest forty-one-year-old I know."

"Thanks. I think."

"Anyway. I'm going to celebrate my birthday this year. Last year, Andy said we'd go out to dinner, just the two of us, and acted all sorrowful when I suggested having a gang of friends over, or going to the pub. And then he cancelled at the last minute. Work. He works pretty hard."

"Even on your birthday." Freya's words were deliberately non-committal.

Carly didn't seem to notice her comment. "This year, though, I'm not going to sit at home all prettied up for nothing. I am going to have fun! We're going to the hotel, girlfriends! Me, you two, and anyone from the yoga class and the sexuality class who wants to come along."

"Count me in." Remy appeared at the table with their coffees. "A girls' night out sounds just the thing."

"No presents, though." Carly picked up the spoon and shovelled three sugars into her coffee, ignoring Freya's disapproving look. "Don't waste your money on a present. Buy me a drink instead."

"When?" Remy tucked the tray under her arm. "And will we go to the public bar, or will you reserve the back room? They let you have it for free if there's more than two hundred bucks put over the bar."

"The back room," Carly decided. "I'll buy the party pies and dim sims from the pub, and I'm sure if there's a dozen of us, we'll get over that two hundred bar tab easy enough."

"How about I bring some vegan nibbles as a contribution?" Remy asked. "Not all of us are junk-eating carnivores like you, Carly." She grinned to take the sting out of her words. "I've done that before. The hotel doesn't mind as long as you let them know ahead of time."

"It's a plan. How about Friday, on my actual birthday?"

"That's good for me," Remy said, and Lily nodded.

"Freya?"

"Sure. That's fine." She squeezed Carly's hand. "And maybe Andy won't have to work late and will come along as well. He can bring his mates too."

"Yeah. Maybe." Carly's fingers worried the napkin, pleating it into a fan and letting it spring back.

Freya sipped her coffee in the silence that followed, her eyes on Carly's down-bent head. She hadn't had a chance to talk to Carly since her confession that things weren't good between her and Andy. Guilt needled her. She should. She would. But Carly was usually so upbeat, her extrovert personality so cheerful, that it had been easy to overlook that Carly was probably suffering inside. She'd ask her around for dinner after her birthday. Just the two of them. She would reconnect with her friend then.

"I'm thinking of getting a cat." Lily looked at each of them in turn. "Dorcas has reminded me how much I miss having an animal. And living so close to her, it wouldn't be fair to get a dog. What do you think?"

"Great idea! Boy or girl cat?" Carly leant forwards, her quietness evaporating. "Get a ginger one. I love ginger kitties."

"That would almost certainly be a male, then." Lily fiddled with the teaspoon. "I really don't mind, though."

"There's a shelter in Mackay." Freya set her mug down. "They have a website, and one of my yoga ladies volunteers there. Do you know Kayla?" At Lily's nod, she continued, "Ask her about cats. The last time she mentioned it, she said they had more animals needing adoption than homes available."

"I'll do that. Maybe I'll go next Monday when the shop's closed and see what they have."

"Can I come too?" Carly's face was alight with eagerness. "I love looking at the puppies. I'd love a dog, but Andy doesn't want one."

"Sure, you can come. As long as you don't come home with an Irish Wolfhound. You won't be able to sneak that in the door when Andy's not looking!"

A crash came from the direction of the kitchen. Remy turned. "Honestly. That new girl is hopeless. Carly, if ever you want to stop being a lady of leisure, you have a job here. I mean it." She disappeared in the direction of the kitchen.

"Does Dorcas get on with other cats? I'm sure the partition between the balconies won't keep them apart. Dorcas comes visiting me sometimes." Lily's gaze rested on Freya's face.

"She used to get on just fine with other cats, but she's been by herself for a long time. I'm sure it will work."

"Good. I'd hate for Dorcas to be upset. That cat is so sweet."

Remy returned balancing three plates. "Brekky wrap for you, Carly. Buckwheat pancakes with apple and cinnamon for Lily, and with banana for Freya."

The pancakes looked fantastic, and Freya's mouth watered. Why had she never tried them before?

"Enjoy your meal. Anyone want another coffee?" Remy asked.

"Yes, please." Carly handed Remy her empty mug, and Lily nodded.

"And I'll see you tomorrow, Lily and Carly. Our second sexuality class. I got a lot of benefit from the first one." Remy winked. "And I need to come into Lily's shop for a look around."

"You do that."

Freya scooped some of the sweet banana. Remy, whom she'd known for years, now appeared to include Lily in the same friendship group as herself and Carly. Maybe it was Lily's city-bred smoothness and confidence—or maybe it was just Lily herself.

"I was in the library the other day." Lily put down her fork. "I saw a poster for a book club. Do either of you go?"

"Not me," Carly said. "They were too earnest for me and seemed to focus on older classics. Freya used to go."

"Not anymore?"

Freya shrugged. "Lack of time, really. And whilst it was good to begin with when there was only a few of us, it went the way of many book clubs: too big, no one could agree on what to read, and too much infighting."

"I was in a book club in Sydney," Lily said. "There were a couple of people who *really* liked the sound of their own voice, if you know what I mean. The last time I went, I think I contributed two words, but the two magpies constantly chattered. I didn't go again."

"There was a bit of that going on with the Grasstree Flat one too. I'm not sure if it's still like that. I haven't been back."

"Lily, you could start one," Carly said. "Didn't you tell me you had a new shipment of books?"

"I did. But it might be a bit limited for most people. The books are either erotic romance, non-fiction, or straight-out erotica. I'm not sure that would be enough to keep a book club afloat. And honestly? I don't have the time. I'm enjoying the bushwalking group; I don't need another indoor activity."

Janie. Lily was probably enjoying Janie as well as the benefits of the great Aussie outdoors. Freya studied her, head tilted to one side. She hadn't seen Janie much lately, certainly not around Lily's shop. Maybe Lily and Janie hadn't been out together. Or maybe they'd spent all their time at Janie's place, where the walls weren't as thin.

A needle prick of something unfamiliar jabbed her guts. Lily and Janie. What would it be like to see them together? A couple? Kissing. She swallowed against a rush of saliva in her throat. Good on them, if they did. Both made no secret of looking for a partner. And she wasn't jealous of Lily. She'd had her chance with Janie, who'd waited a respectable amount of time after Sarah passed before asking Freya out. She'd turned her down firmly enough that Janie hadn't asked again. No, she didn't want Janie.

Freya didn't want anyone.

Chapter 13

"I HAD NO IDEA SO many people would come!" Carly's eyes were slightly glazed in her flushed face. The wine in her glass wavered dangerously close to the rim.

"You have lots of friends." Freya took Carly's glass and set it down before it could spill.

Indeed, most of the women from the yoga class were there, as well as those from other places around town. Including Janie, who was talking intently to Lily. Their bodies were angled towards each other, their conversation focused. Freya turned so Lily wasn't in her direct line of sight. But Lily shifted position, and her patterned orange shirt and dark hair, shining like a raven's wing under the lights, moved back into Freya's vision. Lily moved closer to Janie, and laughed at whatever Janie had said. Lily's laugh was wholehearted—like most everything she did. She threw her head back and her laughter pealed. The woman apparently never censored anything in her behaviour.

Janie put a hand on Lily's forearm and leant in to whisper something in her ear.

Freya turned again so she was facing Carly. "Thirty-five is treating you well so far?"

Carly beamed, a slightly cross-eyed expression. "Yeah. So far, my tits are still sitting high and my wrinkles are no deeper than they were yesterday. Andy found a grey hair, though. He teased me about dyeing it. I told him I'd dye it blue. He didn't find that as funny as I did. He must have thought I meant it!" She reached out an unsteady hand and petted Freya's salt-and-pepper curls. "I'm going to go gracefully grey like you."

One of Carly's friends came up and pressed another glass of wine into Carly's hand. "Happy Birthday," she said, then pecked Carly on the cheek and disappeared again towards the bar.

Carly took a hefty swig of the new glass. "That was good timing. I seem to have mislaid my drink."

Freya eyed the missing drink, sitting in plain view on the table, but didn't say anything. Carly, normally the most moderate of drinkers, was already stonkered. Any more and she would need carrying home. Andy was supposedly coming later; hopefully, he would look after her. In the meantime, Freya would have a quiet word with the bar staff about the responsible service of alcohol.

Carly leant in closer, wobbling on her high heels. "I love you, Freya. You're a great friend. And if I was gay, I would absolutely fancy you." She hiccupped. "Pity in some ways I'm not. Cos if I were, I would hit on you, and on Lily." Her brow furrowed. "Not Janie, though. She's a bit sharp around the edges. Like she's made of razors and bread knives. But Lily… You should absolutely go for her. She's fucking gorgeous. All big and beautiful and so kind. Why don't you, Frey? You can't live like a fucking nun forever." Her voice rose enough that the women next to them turned to look.

Freya wrapped an arm around Carly's shoulders and urged her towards a table. "Why don't we sit for a bit?" She took Carly's wine glass from her and set it down along the way.

"Yeah" Carly wrapped her arm around Freya's waist and allowed herself to be led. "Maybe I've drunk a little too much."

"I'll get you a soft drink." Freya looked around for someone reliable to sit with Carly whilst she was gone. The last thing she wanted was for someone to give her more wine. The room was emptying out; this was still an early-to-bed Queensland town, and ten was a late night for many.

Her scan of the room caught Lily's gaze. Concern furrowed Lily's brow, and she excused herself from Janie and came over. Flashing a smile at Freya, she sat. "How's it going, Carly? This has been a great night. Lots of people here to celebrate your birthday."

"Yeah. It has. Stay and talk with me and Freya." Carly pushed her hair back from her face.

"Of course. But I'm going to the bar for a soda lime and bitters first. Can I get either of you one?"

Carly nodded, and Freya said, "Yes, thank you."

Lily was back in a couple of moments with three pots of the non-alcoholic drink.

"Thanks." Carly clinked her glass against both of theirs. "I was just saying to Freya that if I were gay, I would hit on her. I'd hit on you too, Lil. Just sayin'."

"Thank you for the compliment." Lily squeezed her hand.

"Are you and Freya friends now?" Carly peered into each of their faces in turn. "Good. I like that my friends are friends."

Friend. The word settled into Freya's mind. Lily had offered friendship from the word go. She had never withdrawn that offer, even during their differences.

"Lily's great, Frey. She's taught me lots. About myself mainly, but also she's helped me see clearer about Andy. She knows what to do in bed too. She's taught me a few things about that as well. A woman's pleasure... Her shop is well named. She taught me techniques and stuff, both for me and my lover. She told me it's okay for me to ask for what I want in bed. I can talk to her. Not just about sex, either. Lily listens. Lily knows more about sex than anyone I know."

Freya hunched her shoulders and looked down at her drink rather than at Carly's face. She'd never been one to handle the giggly girl-talk of sex and relationships.

Feet thumped on the wooden boards. Freya looked up at the sound. Andy, face suffused with anger, had appeared behind Carly. He grabbed her arm, his eyes slits in his livid face. "So this is why you lie like a dead fish in bed. You're getting your jollies from your lesbo friends."

Freya opened her mouth to defend Carly. Andy, usually the most affable of blokes, who'd seemed to have no problems with anyone's sexuality, bristled with tension. Carly's jaw hung open and she wrenched her arm from Andy's grip and clung to Lily's arm. Her gaze had snapped back into clarity. In turn, Lily, placed a comforting hand over Carly's.

"Easy, Carly," she said in soft tones. "Don't jump. Now is not the time."

Freya looked from one to the other in bewilderment. Lily's hand on top of Carly's. Carly's fingers clutching Lily's arm. The closeness of their posture, leaning in towards each other, shoulders touching. Lily and *Carly*? Carly, who not ten minutes ago had been proclaiming her straightness and wishing her husband had managed to make her party. And *Lily*, who in those same ten minutes had been getting up close and personal with Janie. Janie, who leant against the bar, staring at the unfolding scene with an expression of bemusement on her face.

Freya shut her mouth with a snap. Something wasn't right here, but she didn't think the obvious scenario was the correct one. She flicked a glance at Andy. Emotion and anger simmered below the surface of the three players in this conversation. Words unsaid, feelings not made clear.

Carly shrugged off Lily's hand and stood. The moment of clarity had passed and she swayed slightly, and put a hand on Lily's shoulder to steady herself. "And what if I am? I have to get some fun somewhere. After all, you're going elsewhere for yours. This kettle calls the pot black."

For a second, Andy's face wore a wide-eyed look of surprise. Then his eyes shuttered and a smile hovered briefly over his lips. "I don't know what you're talking about."

Lily's brow pinched tight between her eyes for a second. "Carly, this isn't a conversation to have when you're drunk."

"I can't think of a better time." Carly's posture straightened, and she lifted her hand from Lily's shoulder to push the hair from her eyes. "Kim. The office manager where you work. The woman you're *fucking*." She spat the word into the noisy room.

Freya jerked in surprise and her gaze flicked to Andy. He stood like a rock, his face still, eyes watchful.

"You think I'm some stupid bimbo who can't put two and two together? Fuck *you*, Andy. I know where your car's been parked. You don't even bother to hide it."

Andy was silent; only the lurid flush above his collar hinted at his anger. "Shut up, Carls. You're drunk. Let's go home."

"Why? So you can talk me around? Tell me Kim keeps the bloody office supplies in her bedroom? Tell me you needed a new fucking stapler?"

Andy's hand shot out and grasped Carly's wrist. "Shut the fuck up now. This is not the time."

"Why?" Carly's voice was shrill. "Or you'll make me shut up? Big brave man."

Freya surged to her feet. "Let her go, Andy." She focused on Andy's large hand, encircling Carly's wrist.

"Gonna make me?"

Lily moved lightly around to Andy's other side. "There are plenty of people here who will make you."

Andy's lips curled in a sneer. "You must be Lily." His finger stabbed at her chest with enough force that she took a step back. "Stay away from my wife."

Carly jerked her wrist, tearing free. "I called your office whenever you worked late. You never picked up."

"And that means I'm having an affair." His laugh grated on Freya's ears. "Get real, little girl."

"Who lives at 14 Wattletree Road? It's not the prime minister."

Her shrill voice was loud enough that the women at the next table fell silent. Remy stared down at the table. Over at the bar, Janie stood alone, her gaze never leaving Lily.

Andy's face had gone still, watchful. His eyes were intent on Carly's face.

"Don't try and deny it." Carly sat abruptly, as if her legs could no longer support her weight.

Her husband turned away without a word.

"Is that it?" Carly's broken cry was loud enough to silence the group of chattering women at the bar. "You're just walking out? Back to *her*?"

Andy turned on his heel and stalked back. "You're too drunk to hold a conversation." His glance flicked over Lily dismissively and settled on Freya. "I'm sure Freya will put up with you for the night if your lover has had second thoughts." He left without a backwards glance.

"Andy, wait..." He ignored Carly's wail. Tears leaked from her eyes to track silent streams down her cheeks. "What have I done? Lily, what have I done?"

"Shush." Lily gathered her into her wide embrace, and stroked Carly's disordered hair. Gone was the effervescent friend Freya knew; in her place was a sobbing, broken woman. Lily caught Freya's gaze over the top of Carly's head. "Let's get her home. I'm not sure if she owes the pub anything, but can you explain that she'll settle up with them tomorrow if so? I'll meet you outside."

Thoughts pounded in Freya's head about the topsy-turvy world of the last few minutes, but she nodded. Right now, getting Carly home was the most important thing. Home to Lily's flat, she presumed. If Carly and Lily were indeed lovers, it was the obvious place. She went over to the bar and arranged for Carly to settle her tab tomorrow. She mentioned to a couple of Carly's friends that she and Lily were taking Carly home. Most nodded; no doubt they had seen Carly's increasing inebriation, if not the fracas with Andy, and drawn their own conclusions. Janie had moved over to talk to Lily, but the conversation seemed short, and when Freya next looked, Janie had disappeared. Good. That was one less drama to deal with.

Carly's sobs disintegrated into sniffles, and even her curls seemed subdued. Out on the street, the three turned towards Freya's and Lily's homes. Carly clutched Lily's arm with one hand and her other found Freya's hand. Linked, they walked along. The only sounds were the swelling cicada chorus and Carly's harsh breathing.

At the shared entranceway to the shops, Freya stopped. "Do you want me to come up for a bit?"

Lily fumbled around in her bag for keys. "Do you have a spare bed?"

The question surprised Freya "No. I have a fold-out futon, but the mattress has lost most of its stuffing. It's murder to sleep on."

"I don't, either." Lily found her keys and jiggled them from hand to hand. "I've a couple of sleeping bags that I could put on the floor. My couch isn't great for sleeping on."

"I'm not a parcel to be handed around," Carly spoke out, too loud in the still night. "If neither of you want me to stay with you, just say so. I'll go and sleep in the park, or something." Her voice cracked.

"Don't be silly, Carly. You can stay with either of us. Your choice. Freya and I are just deciding how to make you comfortable."

"I can share your bed. Either of you. Both of you together." She giggled. "Maybe not yours, Frey. It's only a double. Lily's got a king; we can share that."

"Of course you can." Lily's words were measured, as if she were picking them carefully. "I just thought that after Andy's accusations, you might prefer not to share a bed, in case it gave him ammunition."

"Fuck Andy." Carly's mouth turned down and tears leaked from her eyes once again. "Except I've done that. Now he's fucking Kim and I'm fucking nobody."

"Let's go upstairs rather than debate this in the street." Lily opened the door. "Hang on to the handrail, Carly. The stairs are steep."

Freya shuffled her feet, feeling as if she had been dismissed. A worm of annoyance twisted. Carly was her friend too; she should be the one caring for her now. She took a deep breath, and pushed down the self-pitying thought. Lily was caring for Carly, that was the main thing.

"Seems like you two are set, then." She made her voice bright and breezy, "I'll see you tomorrow."

Carly grabbed her hand. "Come too, Frey. Please." Her voice was a plea of insecurity. "Andy was a dickhead. I'd really like to talk about it with you."

"You have Lily—"

"Please? I could do with the advice of both of you right now." Her deep exhale reeked of defeat. "Oh, and some coffee."

"I'll put the kettle on. Come on up, both of you." Lily's legs, clad in tight-fitting jeans that made the most of her curves, disappeared up the stairs.

Lily's flat was a mess. Piles of clothes were everywhere, as if Lily had dumped her laundry, and stacks of books toppled over on the table. Freya caught a glimpse of a title, *Exercises to Revitalise Your Sex Life*. Her lips thinned; she'd managed to put Lily's ridiculous idea of yoga for sexual wellbeing out of her mind.

Lily came back from the kitchen. "Sorry about the mess. The books are new stock; I was in the middle of checking them off. Do you both want coffee?"

"Yes, please," Freya said. If it was going to be a long night, she would need caffeine.

Lily cleared the table and brought out not only the coffee but some sort of slice. It looked delicious. At least she didn't need to quiz Lily on the ingredients. When they were seated, Lily pushed the sugar over to Carly without her needing to ask.

Freya sipped her coffee. It was not too strong, not too bitter, just the right amount of body. She set her cup down. "You took me by surprise this evening, Carly," she said. "I'm sorry. I didn't realise things had got that bad. I didn't know that you thought Andy was being unfaithful."

"I suspected for a while. He was always working late, always with an excuse." Carly spooned three sugars into her mug and stirred hard enough that the liquid dipped into a whirlpool. "He always called me on his mobile to let me know he'd be late. Yet when he called from work in normal hours, he used the office landline to save his mobile credit. If I ever called *him* at the office on those evenings, the call would go straight to his voicemail and he'd never call back." Her voice morphed into bitterness. "I turned up unannounced once, after he'd told me he had to work late on some project or the other. The office was in darkness. I sat outside and called the office. It went to voicemail." Her shoulders slumped, and she picked at the edge of a thumbnail. "I called his mobile. For once, he picked up. I asked where he was, and he said he was at work, and that there were four of them all beavering away, trying to meet a deadline. I was too upset to challenge him on it, so I drove home. He returned three hours later."

She paused and took a sip of coffee. Tears ran faster from her eyes, and she wiped them away with an impatient hand. "I bought one of those vehicle trackers from the internet and hid it in the boot of his car. I could track it online. Every night he was 'working late', his car was parked at the same address. It didn't take much sleuthing to discover it was where Kim lived."

"How long has it been going on?" Freya ran a finger around the rim of her mug.

"Six weeks now I've known. I didn't know what to do. I was too ashamed to tell anyone."

"You could have talked to me." Freya used her soothing tone of voice, her yoga teacher's voice.

Carly peered at her through the mess of hair over her face. "I wanted to. But I thought you'd give me *that* lecture. I know you mean well, Frey, but the last thing I wanted was for you to tell me how you can never trust a man, and that I would be better off without him."

Carly's words cut deep. Was she that dogmatic, that insensitive? Would she have pressed her own agenda on a friend in need? Freya shifted in her seat, and examined her thoughts. Sure, that would indeed have been what she would have thought, but she would never have said it. No, it wouldn't have been the time or the place. But a needle of pain stuck into her chest because what mattered was that Carly believed she would have, and that was why she hadn't come to her.

She glanced at Lily. "Did you know this?"

Lily took her time before answering. "Some," she said finally. "Carly came to me after the first sexuality class, just over a week ago."

"That's why I signed up for the class." Carly's tears had stopped, but her words were punctuated with sniffs. "I thought if I learnt how to be amazing in bed, I might win Andy back."

Freya bit back her retort: that it was Andy, not Carly, who needed to make amends. She swallowed a too-large mouthful of coffee instead. It scalded her throat.

Was it only then that Lily and Carly had become lovers? That still didn't add up. Carly was so adamantly straight, and that didn't gel with her desire to get Andy to return.

Lily was watching her inner battle, and one corner of her mouth lifted in a tip-tilted smile. "Carly and I aren't lovers," she said. "Andy jumped to the wrong conclusion. Or maybe he just wanted to shift his guilt."

"No way." Carly managed a wobbly grin. "Sorry, Lily, but you're still the wrong gender for me. I guess Andy misinterpreted something I said."

Lily squeezed her hand. "You were saying I was spectacular in bed." Her glance flicked to Freya. "I think you were talking about the sexuality class, but it didn't sound like that to Andy."

"Oh." Carly drew the word out in a long wail of anguish. "I have to explain. I have to find him and tell him—"

"Do you? You accused him of infidelity. It would appear, on the surface, that *he* is the one who should come to *you* and not the other way around." Freya chose her words with care. "You've done nothing wrong; Andy is the one who strayed."

"But he thinks—"

"Does he?" Lily's voice was a beacon of calm, battered by Carly's desperate words. "Or is he seizing on what he thinks he heard as a way of deflecting your anger? From what you said, Carly, you have enough circumstantial evidence to suggest he's having an affair. Enough, certainly, that the onus is on him to tell the truth, not on you to explain a misunderstanding."

Carly sniffed and clutched her mug with both hands. "He's having an affair. I'm sure of it. I couldn't bear to talk about it for ages as it made me sound pathetic, a loser of a woman with no control over her life. But every single time he's worked late, his car has been at *her* house, except for one time, when it was outside The Seafood Palace—the expensive restaurant he always told me was too pricey for us." She set the mug down with a shaky hand and pushed the heels of her hands into her eye sockets. "What should I do? Please, one of you, tell me. You two are the wisest people I know."

Freya met Lily's eyes over Carly's bowed head. She had no idea what was the best thing to say. Her instinct was to put some strength into Carly's spine and tell her to leave the bastard. Once a cheater, always a cheater. But Carly's earlier comment made her hesitate. This wasn't about a set of rules to live by; this was about her friend, who was hurting badly.

"If not for this affair, were you happy with Andy?" Lily spoke to Carly, but her gaze never left Freya's. "Was he your love, your friend? Did he make you laugh? Did he support you? Did you feel loved?"

"I thought all of those things." Carly spoke the words to the tabletop. "But I was living a lie. I must have been. I can't have given him what he wanted."

"Don't blame yourself." Freya hunkered down beside Carly's chair. "Did he ever voice his discontent before now? How could you fix something you didn't know was broken?"

"I just want things to be back the way they were. I thought he loved me. I thought we were happy. We've been trying for a baby. The bastard. He was going to leave me with a baby and go off with Kim."

"You can't know that. You'll need to talk to him," Freya continued. "But before you do, you must decide what *you* want. If you go in without any clear direction, it will be harder."

Lily nodded. "Sort through the evidence. Are you jumping to the wrong conclusion? Could there be some other explanation?"

Carly shook her head, a miserable, defeated gesture. "I tried. I went through every possible explanation from the simple to the utterly bizarre. He could really be working on a project with her, and working from her house is simply more comfortable. Or she's a long-lost half-sister he never knew about." Her laugh held the strained quality of despair. "But none of it makes sense. Why hide something that's innocent? And, too, if it was innocent, he would have turned up for my birthday drinks on time, not nearly three hours late. Last year he didn't come home in time to take me out. That probably means this has been going on for years now."

Freya rested a hand on Carly's shoulder. "You need to sleep on this. It's late; we're all tired. Go to bed." She glanced at Lily, who gave a slight nod. "Sleep as well as you can; don't try to decide what to do now. Just try and sleep. Do you remember the breathing exercise that promotes sleep?"

Carly nodded.

"Try that. And in the morning, the three of us will talk again. Okay?"

"I don't want to sleep alone." Carly's eyes filled with tears again. "Please. I'll just lie awake brooding, thinking of my life alone. Please, stay with me."

"You'll be sharing my bed. I'll find you something to sleep in." Lily stood and picked up the empty coffee mugs.

"Freya too." Carly's voice held an edge of panic. "Please, Frey, will you stay as well? You're my best friend; I would feel better if you stayed too. You're so calm, so reassuring."

"There isn't another bed, Carly. You know that."

"Lily has a king-size bed. That's big enough for all of us. Please. I'll sleep in the middle—I'd prefer that anyway."

"That's not up to me. This is Lily's living space, Lily's bed. She may not want—"

"That's okay with me. It's up to you, Freya, if you're comfortable with the idea."

Freya glanced from Lily, enigmatic Lily, with an inscrutable expression on her face, to Carly, wide-eyed and frantic. The idea felt wrong. She hadn't shared a bed with anyone since Sarah died. Only Dorcas, and sometimes she felt as though even the cat took up too much space. It had been three years now, and every night she stretched out in her double bed alone, relishing the cool feel of the sheets, of the space that was all hers. But this was for Carly; and if it would help Carly to relax, maybe sleep a little, she could do it. "I'll nip home and get ready for bed and come back."

"I'll leave the door on the latch for you," Lily said.

Back in her own flat, Freya brushed her teeth, washed her face, and changed into her flannel pyjamas. The night was humid, and she would doubtless be too warm, but they were the least revealing of all her nightwear. She didn't want to inadvertently touch skin, or impinge upon Carly's space in skimpier clothing.

She looked at her face in the mirror as she subdued her wild hair with a bandana so it wouldn't tickle Carly. This wasn't ideal, but she would do it. For her friend.

Chapter 14

LILY AND CARLY WERE ALREADY in bed when the front door closed quietly. Lily turned onto her side, facing the bedroom door. Carly lay on her back in the middle of the bed, one hand behind her head. Her eyes were open and she stared fixedly at the ceiling.

"Okay?" Lily asked her quietly. "If this is going to be uncomfortable for you, you can say."

"No." Carly's voice was choked, the word guttural. "Please stay."

Freya's slight silhouette appeared in the doorway, and she moved to the bed, raised the sheet, and slid in. She, too, turned on her side, facing the middle. Carly lay rigidly in the centre, her limbs tight to her body. There was plenty of room.

Lily rested a hand on Carly's shoulder. "I'll turn the light out now. Okay?"

"Yeah. Thanks."

The curtains were half-open, and enough light came through the window from the star-filled night. It was quiet outside; Grasstree Flat wasn't a town for noise. A car passed down the main street; a night bird chattered, a dog barked and was swiftly hushed. Lily left her hand resting on Carly's arm so Carly could feel the warmth and support. Freya, too, had elected to sleep facing Carly, and the two of them bracketed their friend like bookends. Lily brought up her knees, careful not to jab Carly with them, closed her eyes, and tried to relax.

Sleeping three to a bed was strange. Lily had only ever done that once before, and that was in her wilder, younger days when three to a bed wasn't for comfort, but for a lot more exciting things. She dragged in a deep breath. Now wasn't the time to revisit that particular scenario, not when she was sharing a bed with her straight and suffering friend, and her antagonistic neighbour.

Freya. Even with her eyes closed, Lily could picture Freya facing her. Her face would be gentler in sleep; those sharp angles and planes, those edges Freya seemed to wrap herself in, would soften as she relaxed. Would Freya's body be lines of tendon and bone, or were there softness and slight curves underneath her clothes? Freya was like whipcord: slim to the point of skinniness. She had an appetite like a bird, eating sparingly of most things.

Freya wasn't conventionally attractive, but she had a crackling energy, a vibrancy, about her that made looking away hard for Lily. She tried, and she often succeeded, but if she had a reason to look—the yoga class was perfect—then Freya drew her eye.

But Freya was out of the dating game, and Lily respected that. She would never ask Freya out, never kiss her after a yoga class, never pin her small body against the wall of her shop and press her own more luxuriant curves against Freya's slight ones.

A pity.

Lily's eyes opened again, to steal one more glance at Freya. She'd expected to find her sleeping, but Freya's eyes were open and their gazes connected. Freya's cool eyes appraised her, no doubt taking in her messy hair and the faded T-shirt she slept in. Lily focused on Freya's face, not allowing her gaze to drop lower, down the slender throat, where a pulse beat slow and steady against her skin. She would not look lower, down to where the collar of flannel pyjamas—too thick for such a warm night—twisted down, exposing prominent collarbones. She most definitely wouldn't look further, to the slight swell of Freya's small breasts. She wouldn't—but she did.

Her gaze snapped back to Freya's face. She'd been sprung; Freya was watching Lily's face, had obviously seen where her wandering gaze had travelled. Lily's lips opened, the words *I'm sorry* forming in her throat. But Freya merely blinked, a slight smile on her lips. Without a word, she turned over and Lily saw only the rise and fall of her thin shoulders. With a sigh, she rolled onto her back and tried to sleep.

Despite her breathing routine, it took a while for Freya to fall asleep. The room was warm, both from the night air and the unaccustomed heat of extra bodies in the bed. She pushed the sheet down around her waist. The thick pyjamas were a mistake. Careful not to disturb the sleeping woman next to her, she worked the top up revealing a strip of skin to the movement of air from the ceiling fan. Her skin still radiated heat; when she put her palm on her belly, it was hot and damp. No. It was more than that. A heat built inside her that had nothing to do with the warm room. A rising of warmth, stealing up from her core into her belly. A twisting spiral that started between her legs and rose, spreading like smoke through her torso. She tried to subdue it, this unwelcome stranger, this physical reaction she hadn't let into her life for a long time. Three years. Not since Sarah had died.

Freya rolled onto her back again, trying not to disturb Carly next to her. It was surely the alcohol that had put Carly to sleep, but a snoring Carly was better than an awake and crying one. Freya pulled her top higher so her entire belly was exposed nearly to her breasts. Sweat prickled her skin, a sheen of dampness that made the thick cloth heavy and sticky. But still the feelings grew. Unfamiliar after so long without, but undeniable.

Want. Need. Desire. Lust.

All the things she had put out of her life for so long came together now in one shaft of heat that pulsed through her.

Lily had done that to her. One look from her huge dark eyes, one sleepy glance from under lowered lashes across Carly's recumbent form, and Freya was lost. Suddenly, she was as helpless in the face of it as a hormone-crazed baby dyke at her first gay bar. The urge to reach over and touch Lily's cheek, press her palm to that smoothness nearly overwhelmed her. She clenched her fingers onto her pyjama top.

As if sensing Freya's discomfort, Lily turned her head. She blinked, and her lips parted into the slightest of smiles. Freya's breath seemed caught in her throat, moving only in the shallowest tide. The heat of Lily's gaze licked over Freya's face, dropped lower as if drawn by wire. But then Lily closed her eyes momentarily, took a deep breath, and when she opened them again, her face was wiped clean of expression, and her eyes were fixed on Freya's face.

But the heat. The flick of fire Lily had tamped in herself transferred itself to Freya, flickered over her skin, fed by the dark eyes locked on her, until Freya was as hot within as without. She willed herself to break the look, to turn away, sever this fine-strung connection that had leapt into existence between them, but she couldn't. Each indrawn breath was shallower and shallower until Freya thought she might faint.

Then Carly twitched and the light jerk of her leg against Freya's gave her the impetus she needed. Her lips twitched into a faint smile before she rolled over to face the wall. But she still couldn't sleep. Her breathing exercises failed her and the room was too hot, too claustrophobic. She alternately cursed Carly for putting her in this situation and projected feelings of love and warmth and healing at her friend.

Sometime later, in the thick darkness of night, Carly jerked to a sitting position and flung back the sheet.

"I'm on fire. I need air." She shuffled down the bed, knocking Freya and Lily in the process, and crawled off the end.

The window was already part open, but Carly went over and heaved it up as high as it would go. The outside air was warm, but there was a slight breeze. Freya raised on one elbow, blinking sleepily.

On the other side of the bed, Lily rolled over. "Whattimeisit?" The numbers shone on the bedside clock. Around three in the morning.

Carly turned to face them. "I'm going to pee. Sorry to wake you. Go back to sleep." The bedroom door closed behind her.

Freya settled back into the bed. "Go to sleep, she says. After her cyclonic exit, she expects us to sleep?"

Lily's gaze settled on Freya's face with a strange intensity. "I was dreaming about you." She propped her head on her hand and continued to stare.

Freya tried to smile, but Lily's compelling gaze had a sombre effect. "Understandable." She tried for a breezy effect, but the word came out stilted. "Things are strange tonight." Lily's presence was doing strange things to her. Maybe it was being in her bed—lying on her sheets, surrounded by the warmth and intimacy of the bedroom—maybe it was just the woman herself. All her earlier desires rushed back, not slowly, finger by finger, but in a tidal surge that picked her up and dropped her on some further shore, where things like want and need and lust were not shunned. A shore she had not visited in a very long time.

And Lily was looking at her in a way that invited exploration. Dark-eyed, slumberous, with a sensual lethargy. Freya exhaled a long draught. She should turn away, go back to sleep. She could make an excuse of finding Carly—who was taking a very long time to pee. She should put Lily down with a cutting comment of fine sarcasm.

But she didn't. "What was I doing in your dream?" Was that her voice, so thick with desire, so low, an invitation in every heavy word?

"I kissed you." Lily didn't break the gaze. "Just once. It was good."

"Did I enjoy it? Did you?"

"Yes." Lily didn't elaborate.

A beat of excitement pulsed in Freya's chest and spread like a shot of brandy to her belly. Before reason could take hold, before she could talk herself out of it, she reached over the expanse of bed Carly had previously occupied. Her fingers traced Lily's upper arm, her neck, her chin, to settle on her lips. Lily's lips parted under Freya's fingers, and her breath warmed the tips. Freya's body followed her fingers, and she moved over the mattress until there was no space between them.

"Was it like this?" she asked, and then she kissed her.

The surprised puff of Lily's breath warmed her mouth, and Lily's lips yielded under hers. Freya traced their shape with the tip of her tongue, slightly bemused that Lily wasn't kissing her back. She pressed harder, and then Lily *was* kissing her back, her mouth opening under Freya's, tongues meeting, her breath hot and sweet, her skin smooth.

Desire slammed into her like a runaway truck. This was the first woman she'd kissed in passion since Sarah, and the memory of lovemaking crashed through her. She shifted closer still, and her fingers entwined in Lily's hair.

The flush of the toilet permeated her mind. Carly. How could she have forgotten? Freya stiffened and pulled back. When Carly came back into the bedroom, the gap between Freya and Lily was a gulf between them.

Without a word, Carly slid back into bed from the foot. She lay on her back and her breath juddered as she said, "Frey? You awake?"

"We're both awake." Lily sat up and turned on the bedside light.

Any self-recrimination Freya might otherwise have felt was lost in the face of Carly's misery.

None of them slept again that night. Instead, they rose and sat outside on Lily's balcony trying to comfort Carly and work out a plan of action. By the time the dawn pushed rosy fingers over the horizon, Freya was reeling with tiredness and the last thing she wanted was to teach her early yoga class.

"Go." Lily gave her a gentle push in the direction of the door. "I'll stay with Carly. And we'll talk later, you and me, yes?"

She nodded. She still had to process the events of the small hours, to mull over what had caused her to act so uncharacteristically—and to figure out her mental strategies so she could be sure it wouldn't happen again.

Chapter 15

LILY'S GAZE KEPT DRIFTING TO the door, her ears alert for the sound of quiet footsteps on the worn boards. She heard the light laughter and murmur of voices as women left the yoga class, and her senses snapped up a notch. She went out to the balcony to see the women get into their cars, or saunter off along the street. Freya was not with them. Hopefully, she would now return. She would come back for Carly, if not for Lily.

Memories of last night's kiss wound around the pathways in her head. A dream Freya kissing her. The real Freya, eyes intent on Lily's face, the soft touch of Freya's fingers on her shoulders, and then the bite of those same fingers into her flesh as dream and reality merged in an unexpected glorious fusion.

Freya had kissed her.

She glanced across at Carly sitting on the couch, pretending to read a magazine. The whole evening had had a hazy unreality to it. Carly, Andy. Andy's unfounded accusations, and Carly's truthful ones—of that she was sure. And Freya. It all came down to Freya.

The kiss they had shared pushed into her mind once more. Would it be repeated, or would Freya run scared? Lily's money was on the second—at least for now.

She glanced at the door once more. It was still stubbornly closed.

To distract herself as much as to support a friend, she bustled around her flat, keeping up a stream of chatter, making cups of tea and providing food for Carly, most of which she pushed aside without touching. The absence of footsteps ascending the stairs spurred her anxiety. Maybe Freya had gone to catch an hour's sleep before opening the shop. Lily smothered a yawn and glanced longingly in the direction of her bedroom with the big bed, still rumpled from the previous night.

Like most shops, Lily only opened in the mornings on Saturdays, so when nine rolled around, she left Carly on the couch staring at the TV and went to open up. Business was quiet, and few customers came by. Every time the tinkle of Indian chimes sounded from the shop next door, her eyes snapped to her own door, and she wondered if Freya was coming in to see her. But at two, when she closed and bolted the door and went back upstairs, there had been no sign of her neighbour.

Lily sighed. What was she expecting? That she and Freya would now fall into a relationship—girlfriends, partners, a U-Haul? Lily snorted. At least the U-Haul was unnecessary. The memory of the kiss burned behind her eyelids. She shouldn't have responded when Freya kissed her. Maybe she'd been too intense, too much too soon. But, she argued, *Freya* kissed *her*. She hadn't broken her promise not to pressure Freya into something she didn't want. She hadn't. Even if it felt like she had.

Carly was still curled on the couch when she came back upstairs later. Lily sat and put a gentle hand on her shoulder. "Hey, how you doing?"

Carly held up her mobile. "Andy called. I didn't answer. I wanted to, but I didn't know what to say. Without you and

Freya to back me up, I'd probably have caved and gone trotting home."

Lily stroked Carly's hair. Even her curls were limp. "Do you want to go home?"

"I don't know. Yes. No. I want everything to be as it was." Her voice ended on an upwards keen.

"It can't be, Carly. Even if you go back, even if he isn't sleeping with Kim, you'll always have this between you now."

"I know." Tears leaked from Carly's eyes, and she dashed them away with the back of her hand. "He is sleeping with her, though. I know it."

"Then you have to decide if you want to fight for him."

Carly sniffed. "I thought both you and Frey would tell me to leave him. That's what Freya would do. What about you?"

She chose her words carefully. "I don't think anyone can say with certainty what they'd do in a situation until it happens to them."

"But it did happen to you. Inga left you for the winemaker."

"That was a bit different. Inga didn't hide anything. Nor did she get together sexually with Cait until after we had split."

"You let her go. You didn't fight. Why not?"

Lily managed a ghost of a smile. "I did. At first, anyway. I sat down and made a list of everything that had fallen apart between us, and how I could make it right."

"That sounds like something Freya would do."

"It was a long list: house cleaning, the intrusion of social media, our working hours and goals—even how we cooked and ate. I like a meal to be an occasion, prepared and cooked with love, eaten with full attention. Inga is a grazer—she nibbles throughout the day."

"Surely that wasn't a marriage breaker?"

"No, but it was one of many things." Lily lifted Carly's feet so she could sit back in the couch, then lowered them into her lap and rubbed them absently. "But when it came down to it, I'd ignored the warning signs for too long. And then it was too little, too late. Inga had moved on, in her mind at least. When I realised that, I had to let her go."

"Just like that."

Lily lifted a shoulder. "I meditated. Tried to discern the right path. It wasn't easy. But when I realised how hard Inga had fallen for Cait, I loved her enough to let her go. I'm not a believer that there is ever only one person for everyone. More there is a person for everyone for as long as it works. For some people, that's a lifetime. For me and Inga, it was four years."

Carly was silent for a moment. "I don't know if Andy loves Kim, or if it's just a conquest. Just sex." Her mouth twisted. "It's never *just* sex, though, is it? It's always sex and love, sex and power, sex and secrets, sex and ego." Carly swung around so her head was on Lily's lap and her tears dampened her loose pants. "I should try falling for a woman."

"Believe me, it's no easier."

"Yeah. And that's not how I am anyway." A few breaths. "Have you seen Freya since she went to yoga?"

"No. But she would have opened her shop."

Carly sat up. "It's closed now, though. Have I done something to upset her? Do I need to apologise?"

"No, I don't think so. She's probably just catching up on some sleep or something around the home."

"I'd like to talk with her."

"Go and knock on the door. She probably would like to talk to you alone."

"Do you mind?"

"Of course not." Lily's smile twisted slightly. "Go. Come back whenever you want, or if you prefer to stay with Freya, don't worry about it. Just stay."

"I'll come back here, if that's okay." Carly fiddled with the hem of her T-shirt. "Can I leave my mobile with you?"

"If that's what you want. What do you want me to do if it rings?"

If it's Andy, answer it and tell him I'm okay. But nothing else. If it's anyone else, it can go to voicemail. You'll see who it is from the caller ID."

"You could just turn it off."

"No. I don't want to speak to Andy, but I want to know if he calls again. A test. But if you have it, I can't be weak and answer."

With the flat to herself, Lily did some yoga on the balcony to make up for missing the morning class, and tidied the kitchen. It was quiet after yesterday's chaos. She settled on the couch with a cup of Assam tea and one of the books that had arrived. She'd always found it easier to sell books to customers if she'd read them herself and could talk about them with pleasure, and it was certainly no hardship to do.

She was deep in an erotic romance when the doorbell rang. It was Carly.

"I told Freya I'd stay here, as your bed's bigger." Carly shuffled in. "I hope that's still okay."

"Sure." Lily set aside the novel and prepared herself for a long debate.

Carly's clothes were rumpled, and huge shadows under her eyes attested to the broken night. "I talked with Freya. She suggested I get away for a few days to focus on what I want. There's a three-day meditation retreat starting tomorrow. She's arranged for me to attend."

"That sounds good." Lily made her voice non-committal.

"Yeah." The ghost of a smile flitted across Carly's face. "I hope being out of Grasstree Flat will help."

Lily moved to the kitchen. "Cuppa?"

"No thanks. I think I need to be outside. Want to walk along the river with me?"

The river moved in a sluggish wide path towards the ocean. They walked along the gravel path that ran across the flood plain, winding through the paperbarks. A crocodile sunned on the far bank, and a couple of blokes fished from a tinnie, but otherwise they saw no one. Lily walked in silence, enjoying the sun on her face, and the fresh clean smell of the air.

They'd been walking for twenty minutes when Carly asked, "Did Andy call again?"

Lily shook her head. "Two of your friends from last night. No one else."

They didn't talk much after that.

Three days passed and the only time Lily saw Freya was at morning yoga. Then, Freya's gaze was remote, her touch on Lily's spine impersonal as she corrected a pose. Lily tried to catch her eye, force some acknowledgment from her, but Freya's glance slid away like iced water.

Twice, Lily found herself at Freya's shop. The first time, she went away without entering. The second, she went in, but Freya was busy serving a customer.

"Won't be a moment," she said, and continued suggesting alternatives from the range of soaps and lotions.

Lily loitered, but when, after ten minutes, the customer was still there, she returned to her own store without a word.

Freya was avoiding her. And whilst Lily could understand why, the longer it went on, the more she despaired of them returning to their former friendship.

And more.

The kiss they had shared haunted Lily. It ran through her head, waking her in the middle of the night, breathless with kisses from the dream Freya. Freya's lips demanding on hers, her tongue seeking entrance.

Without Carly to act as a comforting buffer, Freya seemed to melt into the walls, so seamlessly was she able to evade Lily. After yoga on the third morning, Lily draped her towel around her neck and wandered in a seemingly careless fashion over to Freya, who was talking to another pupil.

She put her hand on Freya's forearm. "Sorry to interrupt—are we still having coffee this morning?"

The silvery eyes shot shards in her direction. "Sorry, I can't now."

Lily waited for the reason behind the polite excuse, but Freya had already turned back to her pupil. There was nothing else to say.

The walls of her shop were crowding her; the space which normally seemed so welcoming was suddenly claustrophobic. Freya prowled around, tweaking a wall hanging into place, rearranging the display of scented candles, only to move them back on her next pass. Her muscles twitched restlessly with the need to move, and her mind screamed out for uninterrupted solitude. Processing time. Her mouth quirked upwards wryly. What lesbian didn't need that?

When the shop closed, Freya grabbed a water bottle and went down to the river. The sun was still a couple of hours from setting and there was still plenty of heat in the day. The path ran for five kilometres along the river, through the paperbarks and banksias before following the upper bank through grazing land. Freya marched purposefully, the sun hot on her shoulders, letting the exercise clear her head. At first, there was just the static blur of anxiety that no amount of deep breathing could clear. The building blocks that formed her life since Sarah had died, that had seemed so solid, so immutable, were crumbling, falling into dust. Not instantly, but piece by piece. A smile, a shared experience, a moment of understanding—Lily's presence was in all of these. And a kiss.

Her mind shied away from that, and she pushed her feet faster, until she was nearly running. Her singlet was damp with sweat, and her hair escaped the bandana to fall over her eyes. Impatiently, she pushed it away.

How dare she? How dare Lily blow into her life with her brightness and sunshine and laughter? Why did she pick this small town to stir up the cocktail shaker of Freya's life, making friends so effortlessly, running workshops that should have been shunned, but that were very definitely not.

And, how dare she be interested in Freya? How dare she persist in dragging Freya into her life?

She broke into a full run, her feet flying along the gravel path, through the peeling paperbarks, the red jewels of banksia flowers. Her breath rasped in her throat, and her chest ached with the effort, but she forced her muscles onwards, ever onwards, faster, faster, as if she could outrun the confusion in her mind.

She rounded a corner to find a carpet python, its thick body stretching the full width of the path. She cleared it with a flying leap, and the shock of landing dislodged the tears that blurred her eyes and sent them cascading down her cheeks. Her muscles screamed in protest, and sweat and tears mingled in her eyes until she could hardly see.

Freya dropped back to a jog, and then a walk, before coming to a halt, her hands pressed against the red trunk of a gum tree. Her throat was thick with tension, and her feet hurt from running in sandals. Her lungs couldn't draw in enough of the humid air, and her head spun in a grey wave of dizziness. She crouched before she fainted and closed her eyes.

When had it come to this? She had rebuilt her life since Sarah died, and she was content. She didn't need the upheaval. Deliberately she summoned Sarah's face in her mind, not Sarah as she was in the months before her death, but the Sarah of the years before that: serene, gentle, radiating a kindness and empathy. Sarah and her, lying together in the bed where Freya now slept alone, making love with tenderness and passion. *Making love.*

She knew exactly when that had ceased being a part of her life.

Freya rose and turned back the way she had come. She dawdled, letting her feet find their own pace. And whilst her eyes traced the flight of a lorikeet landing in the trees and her fingers crushed the leaves of a lemon myrtle so she could smell the sharp scent, her mind sifted through the memories and resistance.

Memories of love. Resistance to change.

Freya stood aside to let a small child pass, wobbling on his too-big bicycle. His father, running behind, smiled his thanks, and Freya resumed the walk for home. Her life felt like that child; trying for something bigger, but on the verge of disaster. But that child had his father to catch him.

Freya stopped at the end of the path. From here, her shop was visible at the start of the sweep of the road into the main part of town. There was her grey-green door, the planters of flowers on the footpath, and her row of Buddhist prayer flags hanging limply in the still air. Her gaze switched to Lily's shop next door. The silver-and-purple shopfront with the curly wording of the name was tasteful, she had to admit that. Lily had changed the window display. The mannequin was gone, as were the bunches of lingerie. Now there were piles of books, and a French maid's costume, draped over a wooden chair. The effect was more arthouse than sex store.

Freya reached the shared porch just as the door to Lily's flat opened. Lily came out, empty shopping bags in her hand. Freya stopped. There was nowhere to duck out of sight, nowhere to go except into her own shop.

"Hi." Lily smiled and her gaze focused on Freya's face. "I'm off to get groceries. Do you need anything?"

Freya shook her head. "Thank you for asking, but there's nothing I need." *Nothing, except some peace of mind.*

"No worries." Lily swung the shopping bag. "I'll be home later if you fancy joining me for a glass of wine?"

Freya's pulse pounded. The semblance of equilibrium gained from her time by the river vanished in the flash of Lily's dark eyes. "Thank you," she managed. "But I need to prepare for a workshop."

Lily nodded, as if she expected the answer. "Another time soon, then. We need to talk, Freya. Please don't run from me."

"I won't." Even as her feet carried her to her door, she acknowledged the lie.

Carly's return eased the tension. She arrived back the next day and blew straight into the third sexuality class a few minutes late, dumping a sports bag in the corner of the room. Lily smiled a greeting as Carly slipped into her usual seat near the front.

When the class had finished, Carly waited back.

"How was the retreat?" Lily studied her friend. Carly looked more alive than she had a few days prior and she had a ghost of a smile on her face.

"Really good. Helpful. Would you mind if I stayed with you again tonight?"

"No worries. Do you want me to ask Freya over?"

"Up to you. I don't need to talk, if that's why you're asking."

Carly followed Lily up to her flat and threw the bag on the couch. Lily poured wine, and Carly sat on a stool watching as Lily prepared dinner.

"I'm going to ask Andy to have coffee with me tomorrow," she said. "Not at Remy's place—too many long ears. Down at Oncey-One's. No one I know goes there."

Lily nodded and waited.

"I don't want him back. Not now anyway." Carly took a mouthful of wine before continuing. "Once a cheater, always a cheater. And things weren't that good for a long time. I don't want to start the cycle I've seen happen to others: he swears he'll never do it again, I take him back, for a while things are good, and then he starts up his old patterns again, and before I know it, I'm once more sitting at home alone crying into my wine."

"Where will you go? You're welcome to stay here for as long as you like. I can get a futon and you can have some space in the living room."

"Thank you, but no. I don't want to impose. It's time I made a new start, and that means living alone for the first time in my life. I went from my parents' place to shared housing at uni, and then I married Andy. I'm going to get a flat here in town. I'm seeing one tomorrow, over on Fielding Street. And I'm getting a job. Actually, I've already got one. I'm going to take Remy up on the offer to waitress for her."

"Is that what you're going to tell Andy?"

"Yeah. I don't know if I can do this, to be honest. I'm afraid I'll see him, and all the feelings I had for him will come rushing back. But I know I have to try." She reached out to Lily, touched her hand as she pulled a lettuce apart for salad. "I see you being so free, so unattached. Sleeping with whomever you want. And I see Freya, wanting no one, *needing* no one. Just living her own life. And I think if the two of you can do it, then surely I can too."

Lily swallowed. Carly's words felt like a half-truth, as if she were only seeing part of the picture, the outward parts Lily and Freya presented to the world. The sexual free-spirit and the empowered asexual being.

"I was married, Carly. Don't forget that. And if Inga hadn't left me, I'd still be in a monogamous relationship."

Carly was silent, studying her. "If you found the right person now, a woman whom you loved and she loved you back, would you commit to her?"

"In a heartbeat." Lily put down the lettuce and leant across the counter. "Carly, I teach sexual freedom and expression, and I truly believe it is a natural joyous thing. And yes, I've had partners since Inga left. Probably less than you believe. But I would still commit to a monogamous relationship with the right woman. So I guess what I'm saying is follow your heart.

Don't follow my path, or Freya's, just because you think it's what you should do."

"Thank you. But I have to try and be by myself. And I'm testing him, I know that. I'm not so confident when it comes down to it. If he shrugs and goes off with Kim, then it doesn't say much, does it? So I guess this is as much about seeing what he will do when he's supposedly got more freedom. Maybe that's the wrong way to go about it. Maybe I should demand he returns and is faithful."

"Ultimatums seldom work in relationships. They so often backfire."

"And forcing someone to adhere to something that deep down they don't want, seldom ends well." Carly nodded. "When did I become so wise?" Her face crumpled. "Lily, I don't know what I want in the long term yet. But I have to determine that alone. Not living with Andy." She took a deep breath. "Thank you for the support you've given me. You and Freya."

"Anytime."

"Change of subject." Carly's grin was an approximation of her former exuberant one, but it was a start. "So are you and Janie an item now?"

Lily turned to the fridge to find the tomatoes so Carly wouldn't see her face. "Janie? No."

"Not even for fun?"

"Janie's lovely. But I don't think she's right for me." She set the tomatoes on the counter and returned to the fridge for capsicum.

"Oh." Carly snatched a couple of cherry tomatoes. "Then who is? Not Freya, obviously. You can relax; no more matchmaking from me. You're obviously not suited."

Not Freya. The one woman who had occupied her mind in one way or another since Lily had moved to Grasstree Flat. Carly was right in that respect. Or was she?

"Why do you think we're not suited?" Her voice was muffled by the fridge. "You were trying hard enough to get us together not long ago." She straightened and arranged her face in a neutral position.

"I guess because you're so different. Personality wise. I thought you would be a good match as you have interests in common, but it's not enough. You and Janie share many interests, and your approach to life is similar."

"Was Freya always the way she is? What was she like with Sarah?" Lily clenched her jaw against the rest of the words.

"Sarah was one of those shining people, you know the sort? Softly spoken, gentle, and the goodness shone out of her like the sun. Never had a bad word for anyone." Carly's face softened in remembrance. "She sounds like a pious saint when I put it like that, but being around her was a lift to the spirits. And she loved life. Loved sex, too, from what she said. Sarah was touchy-feely. Always a hug, a touch, a kiss on the cheek. Freya was more like that too back then, but she always had that reserve about her. But since Sarah died, Freya's closed in, folded over on herself, got more into this 'strong, independent woman' thing." She bit her lip. "Right now, I wish I were like that."

"You said it earlier, Carly. You have to be yourself."

Carly poured more wine. "I keep thinking Freya will move on. Find someone to love again. But she's rebuffed the people who tried. Janie, for example. Now, I think she just wants friends."

Friends. A couple of weeks ago, she too would have said being friends with Freya was enough. Now she wasn't sure.

Chapter 16

THE MORNING LIGHT STREAMED THROUGH the windows along the side of the studio as Freya led her pupils through the poses. If she were honest, this intermediate class was her favourite. Most of the pupils had been with her for at least a couple of years and had come up through her beginner classes. They were knowledgeable enough to require little direction, yet fresh enough that there was joy in their movements.

And there was Lily.

On the surface, Lily's movements were as assured as the other women's, her large body moving with grace and smoothness. She knew what she was doing, and her pleasure in the class was obvious. Freya's gaze moved around the room. Remy had hurt her back in the café a few days before and her movements were jerky as she tried to compensate for the pain. Freya touched her hip, urging her into a better position. Miriam wobbled in eagle pose, and touched a toe to the floor to steady herself. A quick smile at her clumsiness and Miriam resumed.

Freya reached the rear of the room and studied Lily. She, too, was in eagle pose, one bare foot hooked around the other calf, her hands wrapped around each other, level with her face.

Her pose was rock solid, her face serene. Freya's teeth clenched. How could Lily be so calm, so steady, when Freya's own world was rocking so precariously?

"Centre yourself," she said, the words an abrupt snarl. She adjusted the position of Lily's hands with unnecessary roughness.

Lily moved her hands, but the twist of her mouth and her slow blink told their own tale.

She was being unfair. Lily's silent obedience sent a coil of shame into her belly. She was above such pettiness—or she tried to be. She returned to the front of the room and moved into king dancer pose, which was new to this group. As she looked around the room, at the wavering balance and ragged shapes in front of her, the twinge of shame grew. The only person holding an approximation of correct form was Lily. Their eyes met across the room, and the hint of a smile on Lily's face broadened.

Freya's mouth snapped shut. She would not give Lily the satisfaction of correcting her hip position.

If the class ended a few minutes early, no one called her on it. If Freya's bowed head and *namaste* was more hurried than usual, no one commented. When the last of the class had departed, Freya turned back to the room with a sigh. Her shoulders slumped in relaxation, but the headache twinging at her temples continued to pound. She stood tall, and breathed relaxation into her body, seeking to regain the calm of the morning. Each breath poured equilibrium back into her mind. When she opened her eyes again, she came face-to-face with Lily's dark gaze.

They stared at each other, eyes locked, their breathing slowing, synchronising, until the rise and fall of their chests found a matched rhythm.

"I thought you'd left." Freya couldn't look away, couldn't break the connection that strung between them, fine as silver leaf, strong as steel.

"I wanted to thank you for the class." Lily's words formed into the air with agonising slowness. "I enjoy your classes. You're a good teacher."

"Thank you. I'm glad you continue to attend."

"Is there any reason I shouldn't?"

Was there? If there was, it was only in Freya's head.

"No."

Lily moved closer, into Freya's space, and lifted her fingers to twist a strand of Freya's hair. "You're avoiding me."

"I'm not." Even as the words sounded, Freya recognised the lie.

The corner of Lily's mouth lifted in amusement, but she didn't say anything.

"You're right. I was."

One of Lily's fingers brushed Freya's cheek as she curled the hair around again. "You don't have to, you know. I don't want to make you uncomfortable. I love...what we're forming."

What were they forming? The ache in Freya's head pulsed anew. "I shouldn't have kissed you. It was wrong."

Lily's eyes held kindness and understanding. "I disagree. It felt very right to me." She took a tiny step forwards, and her fingers curved around the back of Freya's neck. "It felt wonderful." Her breath was warm on Freya's lips.

Freya's breath was a shallow tide and her feet planted heavy on the floor. Sweat sheened her skin in the warm room.

"It felt like this."

And then Lily's lips touched hers, once, twice, light touches that were barely there, only enough to start the slow and lazy burn. Lily drew back and took a deep breath, and in a lightning bolt of knowledge, Freya knew she was going to kiss Lily again, really kiss her, a take-no-prisoners, all-or-nothing kiss. She inhaled sharply.

The door banged and footsteps moved to the back of the room. "Don't mind me." Alicia, one of her pupils, darted to the bench. "Left my phone behind."

Freya's cheeks heated and she took a step back. Her chin lifted, and she turned to say something to Alicia, but she had gone. The door banged a second time, this time behind her.

"Don't." Lily's fingers found hers. "Don't retreat from me. Please."

"I have to go." Freya straightened her tunic, worried the hem with her fingers.

"Come to dinner with me. Later."

"I really don't think that's a good idea."

"Please. I've grown used to eating with Carly. Now that she's moved into her flat, it will be strange eating alone."

"All right, then." The words came up unwillingly, but once said, the idea seemed pleasant.

"Great." Lily's smile competed with the sunlight coming in through the wide doors. "Around seven?"

She nodded.

Climbing the stairs to Lily's apartment had a familiarity to it, her feet automatically knowing the best place to step on the worn treads. Of course, she had come this way several times when Diane had run the veggie shop, but it was never to spend time in the evening, only for business matters, something that related to both their shops.

She found Lily on the balcony. Dorcas in her lap. The cat purred, and looked up at her owner through half-closed eyes.

"She appeared less than a minute ago." Lily smiled up at Freya, even as she stroked the cat's fur with her fingers. "She must have waited until you left before coming over." Lily set Dorcas to one side. "Let me get you a glass of wine."

The balcony bore evidence of Carly's whirlwind presence. Despite her now having moved into her own flat, a pair of her yoga pants was on the couch, some junk food packets and a couple of dog-eared self-help books on the table.

Lily returned with the wine, and clinked glasses. "To us," she said. "The wider us. Our friends, our shops."

Freya swallowed. She'd agreed to dinner, and with dinner, the expectation of moving forwards. But panic roiled. She wasn't ready. Maybe she never would be. If she closed her eyes, Sarah was behind her closed lids. It was too fast, too soon. Would this terrible locking in her throat ever leave? She couldn't say the words Lily wanted: *to us—together*. She sipped and put her glass down on the table to cover the silence.

"I went to the animal shelter." Lily looked across to where Dorcas stretched out on more than half the couch. "I've signed the papers to adopt a mature cat. There were lots of sweet kittens, but I fell in love with Mabel. She was all by herself in a cage, hiding underneath one of the perches. The shelter staff said she'd belonged to someone who'd died, and none of the family were able to take her. I couldn't pass her up. She eventually came over to me when I coaxed, but she looked so sad. She's used to other cats, so I hope Dorcas and she will get along."

"When does she arrive?"

"It might be a few days. The shelter vet wants to be sure she's healthy before releasing her for adoption. She's the cutest little grey-and-white cat. Very small."

"I'll keep Dorcas indoors for a couple of days when she arrives. That way Mabel can get used to the balcony and surrounds without Dorcas landing on top of her."

"Thanks. That's a kind thought." Lily gestured to the living area. "I'm just going to do a couple of things in the kitchen. Come and talk to me if you want."

Freya followed Lily into her compact kitchen and perched on a stool, watching as Lily sliced tomatoes and avocado for salad. "I missed Carly at yoga this morning. Have you seen her?"

"She only moved into her flat yesterday. I haven't seen it; she was adamant she would do it by herself. Well, her and a removal van. I was giving her some space. She's rather lived in my pocket the last few days."

"She invited me around for coffee tomorrow. Are you going?"

"No. I've got my sexuality class later that day, and I'm behind in preparing for it, so I said some other time."

"Is Carly still attending?"

"She said she would." Lily slanted her a sideways glance. "There's room in the class if you want to attend. Tomorrow, we're going to be diarising as expression."

"I run a similar class already." Her words were stiff. Every time she talked with Lily, Lily seemed to encroach more insidiously into her space, her area of expertise.

"This is *sexual* expression. Anything people find difficult to say out aloud. Whether it's individual words, or a fantasy, or even a difficult experience they want to express so as to relieve the burden. People can write it down, share if they are comfortable with that, or else take it home. Maybe even burn it to free themselves from the experience." Lily put down the knife and smiled at Freya across the counter. "You are welcome to come, Freya. If you want. It's a form of letting go."

The additional words *of Sarah* hung in the air.

Freya's gaze slid away, around the cosy kitchen. It wasn't the first time someone had suggested something like this. The counsellor she'd seen after Sarah's death, her friends: they had all suggested some version of sharing.

"If you want to move on." Lily looked down at the tomato.

Freya's nails dug into her palm. The presumption in the sentence wormed under her skin where it nicked and pricked like a sandfly.

"I'll pass, thanks. I don't think I would benefit."

Lily studied her, as if calculating the best response. Then she grinned. "Aw, c'mon, Freya. It could be fun. It's not all sombre seriousness. There's a couple of people who take the light-hearted approach every time." She leant forwards. "Between you and me, I suspect their secrets are buried too deep to come out in a semi-public setting, even one as supportive as my class, but that's okay."

"Thanks, but no." She picked up a cracker, and spread it with the dip Lily had placed on the table. "This is good. Did you make it?"

"Yes. It's a recipe Inga used to make all the time. Just one of the good things to come from that relationship. What did you take away from your relationship with Sarah?"

Freya's eyebrows lowered at the casual familiarity. "Cashew nuts, rocket, olive oil, pepper… What else is in this dip?"

"Tofu and lemon juice. You didn't answer my question."

"I don't wish to. Not everyone wants to shout their secrets to the sky. Not everyone is comfortable doing that. And not everyone wants to move on. Life isn't made up of cookie-cutter pieces that all fit together. There isn't a way forwards that everyone has to take, and that includes your bloody class." Her teeth ached from grinding them, and her throat was thick—with anger or tears, she couldn't tell. Right now, they were one and the same.

Lily's face washed clean like the morning after a storm. She tilted her head to one side. "No. But having someone to talk to can be good."

"I have friends to talk to. I don't need a bloody class of giggling women."

"Then talk to your friends. Carly is as closed as a clam when you come up, but I get the impression you don't talk to her. Nor Remy."

Her lips pressed together and she tasted blood. "You are not my counsellor. You and your damn class."

"You're scared." Lily busied her hands with the knife, turning it over in her fingers. "That's okay; it's not easy."

"Leave me alone. Stay away. Stop interfering. I don't need you or your help."

Lily radiated calm. "I will. If that's what you want. But only after you've come to one of my classes. Fair play, Freya. I come to yoga—"

"It's not the same."

"No. But on so many levels, I wish you would come. You're my neighbour. You've yet to give me an answer on running a sex-and-yoga class together. Come along and call it research, if anyone asks you. Or I'll say that's why you're there. Or come because you think it might help you in some way. None of my other ladies are afraid to admit that. You can too. It's helped me in the past; I think it can help you."

"I don't need any help. And if I did, I'd go to a professional."

"But you don't go."

"Because I am happy with my life. You got over your heartbreak by becoming this free sexual being, or whatever you call yourself. No worries. I'm not judging you for that. But that's not what I will do. Or want to do." She stood. "This conversation is at an end. Thank you for the wine. Keep dinner. I don't want it."

Lily stood, too, so that they were eye-to-eye, the counter between them. "One class. Call it research. Call it what you damn well want. One class, and then if you don't like it, I'll leave you alone."

"I don't have to prove anything to you."

Soft clucking noises issued from Lily's throat.

Freya turned away and stalked to the top of the stairs. "And stay away from my cat!"

Chapter 17

LILY HADN'T EXPECTED FREYA TO turn up to the class. After the challenges she'd thrown at her during their aborted dinner, Lily had expected Freya to retreat to the sanctuary of her shop, her flat, and yoga. But when she entered the studio, Freya was already there, slightly apart from the other women, sitting as stiffly as it was possible to do in a beanbag. A ring-bound notebook and pen rested on her lap.

Lily nodded to everyone, and reminded them about the tea, coffee, and soft drinks at the back. She glanced about her. Nine women. It was about five more than she'd hoped to get when she'd first floated the idea of this class. Remy, Carly, Janie, and other women from the town, most of them in their thirties or older. And Freya.

She kept herself apart, avoiding eye contact and replying to her friends' comments in monosyllables. Carly went and plopped in the beanbag next to her, forcing Freya to squish over. Carly slung an arm over Freya's shoulders and whispered something in her ear. If anything, Freya tensed even more.

"Writing." Lily smiled around the room. "It's your brain to the pen or keyboard. There's nothing in between. Many writers say there's a special connection to their fingers that bypasses conscious thought. They might look back on a piece of writing and wonder where it came from as they don't remember the process of putting the words down. This class is all about letting go of the filters that stop your voice. Sometimes, by getting those words out, you can make them reality—or let them go. But acknowledging them is the first step."

The women shuffled and there was a high-pitched giggle from Remy, abruptly silenced.

"No one will read what you write here, unless you choose to share it. No one. Not me. Not the woman next to you. This communion is between you and the page—or laptop."

"I've tried this." Janie piped up from where she sat at a table, her tablet in front of her. "And every time I end up staring at a blank screen, my mind a fizzing mess of nothing."

"You don't have to find the perfect sentence to start with. Sometimes, just the act of writing starts the process. You can start with a grocery list if you want and let it morph into wherever it takes you."

Carly heaved herself from the beanbag and went over to sit with her back to the wall. "I'll get started. I've got a lot to process."

The class fell quiet. Lily walked around, standing close to each woman in turn. Far enough away that she was clearly respecting their privacy, but near enough that they could ask a question if they wanted. Her own notebook and pen, resting open on her desk upstairs, tickled at her mind. She had tried this exercise herself. The single page of doodles and embellishments around a single name told their own story.

She wiped clean her own obsessive thoughts, and concentrated on her class. Eight of the nine women were busy writing, or typing fast on a laptop. The ninth woman sat frozen and apart, her gaze remote.

Lily went over and squatted near the beanbag. "Try and clear your mind. Then when you are centred, visualise one word that encapsulates what you want to write about. It could be a name, a heading, a trigger word."

Freya nodded, her movement a jerky up and down. Her fingers clenched on the pen but didn't move.

"Try closing your eyes." Lily moved closer, enough that she could see the blank page in front of Freya.

Freya shot her a glance but remained silent.

"What do you think is stopping the flow?" Lily knelt and clasped her hands on her own thighs.

Freya's look lanced her with scorn. "What do you think? I didn't want to come in the first place."

Conscious of the nearby women, she kept her voice low. Soothing. "Why did you come, then?"

Freya turned the pen end to end. "Carly made me."

"You don't strike me as someone who does anything simply because someone else persuades you. You're here now. Why don't you try. Let it all flow." She placed her hand over Freya's, stilling the jerky movement on the pen. She prised first one, then the rest of her fingers loose and took it. After turning Freya's pad to face her, she wrote one word in block letters on the top: *Sarah*.

Freya's breath hissed. "You presume to tell me what I should do?" Her eyes narrowed to slits, like Dorcas focused on a cockroach.

"No. It's only a suggestion." She took the pad again and wrote another word: *Lily*.

Freya's laughter grated harshly. "Dream on."

"I won't read it."

"You won't get the chance." Freya snatched the pen back and started scribbling on the page. Words formed and flew from her pen. "Isn't there anyone else who requires your assistance?"

Lily stood. The dismissive glance that came her way warmed her. A reaction, that was what she wanted and that was what she had got. She paced over to where Carly sat against the wall, muttering under her breath.

Freya was participating, albeit unwillingly. She glanced back to where Freya sat. As if her gaze had touched her, Freya's head came up and her gaze locked on Lily. The grey eyes were distant, as if revisiting another place, or another time. There was a softness in them, one Lily had seldom seen.

The heaviness in her chest caught her by surprise. Of course, Freya was reminiscing about Sarah: beautiful, perfect Sarah, who even though she had passed three years ago, still held sway on Freya's emotions.

What would it take to get Freya to look at her, Lily, like that?

She turned away. Probably nothing on this earth.

Lily allowed twenty minutes of writing time. Although she watched everyone, one eye on the clock, her gaze kept drifting back to Freya. Her head was bent, and pages covered with a neat, tight hand rested beside her.

When the allocated time had passed, Lily cleared her throat. "Time's up. Gather up your things and come back to the front."

Her attention was taken by Remy who, in standing, dropped her notebook. Loose-leaf paper flew everywhere. When Lily next cast her glance around the room, Freya had gone. She had vanished as softly as early mist on the river.

"What did you all take from those last few minutes?" she asked. "Who wants to start?"

Carly followed her up to the flat after class without an invitation. Lily put the kettle on and turned to study her friend. Carly's face was pinched, and despite the relaxation of the previous hour, tension radiated from her. Lily made coffee and pushed the sugar bowl closer.

"How are you doing?" she asked.

Carly's lips twisted in an approximation of a smile and her eyes were bleak. "Okay, I guess. Andy won't let me into the house. He claims I need to call first before I come around. It's half my house, Lil. At least the bit the bank doesn't own. That has to count for something."

"It does." Lily busied her hands with her own mug. "Your contribution to the home may not have been monetary, but it was a major one."

"I don't think he's seeing Kim any more, though. The tracker is still working in his car—he can't have found it—and his car hasn't been at her house now for a few days. Not that that really means much. There are other places: desks, office kitchens, the park, the beach..."

A mental image of Andy ripping his car into pieces to look for the tiny device made Lily smile.

"Have you talked? Really talked?"

"He shouts and I snipe. Is that talking?"

"Not for this purpose."

Carly pushed her mug to one side and dug the heels of her hands into her eye sockets. "I want him back. I know, you don't need to tell me. I've heard it all from so many people. Once a cheater, always a cheater. I'll never be able to trust him again. We'll have the baby we've been trying for and he'll leave me high and dry, with a big baby belly and a ruined body, and he'll be back eating in fancy restaurants with Kim, whilst I beg him for child support."

"Would he do that?"

Carly's words were muffled by her hands. "I wouldn't have said so. Before. Andy was the nicest guy. Caring. Considerate. He loved me, I'm sure of that. It's only the last few months that he's been distant."

Lily was silent. This wasn't something she could do for Carly.

"I know, you don't need to tell me how stupid I am, wanting him back. I get that from everyone else. Freya—"

"Freya?" The word was sharp.

"Oh, she hasn't told me I'm batshit insane, hasn't lectured me about becoming a strong and independent woman. She doesn't need to. She's been nothing but supportive of my choices. But I know, deep inside, that's what she's thinking. Because that's how she is. At least, that's how she *wants* to be: a woman who needs no one. But I wish she wasn't like that. I'd love to see her in love again. Happier." She blinked. "When did we get to talking about Freya?"

"I'm not going to tell you you're stupid." Lily couldn't think about Carly's later words. "But I am going to tell you that you need something from Andy before going back to him. Some sign of remorse, of willingness to change."

"I know. So that it doesn't just return to how it was: me at home, him whooping it up with Kim."

The evening stretched long and introspective in front of Lily. "Do you want to stay for dinner?"

"Do you mind? I was going to ask you if I could stay over. I don't think I'm the sort of person who can live alone. That flat of mine seems so lonely, so sad. Creepy even."

"That's okay."

"Thanks. I'll sleep on the couch if you want your bed to yourself."

Lily stood and moved over to the fridge. "I don't mind if you don't."

"Thank you. I drove over. My overnight bag is in the car." Her expression was sheepish. "I presumed it would be okay to stay. I'd ask Freya, but I think she needs some space after your class." She grinned, a spontaneous expression that was nearly back to her old self. "Freya can be scary sometimes."

Lily pictured Freya's fierceness, her antagonism, and her willingness to stand with a friend. "You're right." But the softer Freya intruded. The caring person, the serene and grounded woman. The lover?

Right now, that seemed too big a leap.

Lily didn't come to yoga the next morning. Although the other women were there, the room felt empty without her colourful presence at the back. Freya missed her curvy shape, in bright leggings and oversized T-shirt, performing the poses with an innate grace and calm.

Lily skipped the next class too, and the one after that. When Lily had started attending, Freya figured she'd last a week, two at the max. But it was months, not weeks, now, and Lily had seldom skipped. Freya knew Lily hadn't gone away. Her shop still opened punctually at nine, and she heard the occasional snatch of salsa through the wall in the evening.

Freya ticked off the attendees each class, and when four days had gone by with blank boxes by Lily's name, there was only one conclusion: Lily was avoiding her.

She missed her. Missed her rich chuckle as she exchanged a word with one of the other women, missed the way her eyes fluttered closed as her chest rose and fell with the rhythmic, slow breaths of meditation. And she missed the pleasure of her full body moving with a practiced flexibility that put many of the younger, slimmer women to shame. She missed, too, the way her breasts pressed against the T-shirt, and the soft curve of her lips in an upwards arc. Lily always looked like she was smiling, even when her face was relaxed and soft.

Then Carly skipped a class. Freya had seen her a couple of nights before. They'd gone for a walk along the river in the relative cool of evening. And then they'd gone back to Carly's new flat, which was simply furnished with mismatched pieces from the op shop, as if Carly was yet to believe it was home. Carly had skated over the question of how she was settling in. She hadn't said she wouldn't be at yoga, nor had she said she wouldn't make breakfast. Freya went along to the Green House anyway and ate a solitary bowl of chia-and-pecan porridge.

"What, no more buckwheat pancakes?" Remy said, and Freya shook her head.

She returned home earlier than usual. With no Carly to chat with, dragging it out seemed pointless. Back in her own flat, she put on the kettle, and heard the laughter through the shared wall. Laughter and voices: Lily's and Carly's. It sounded as if they were having breakfast.

Without her.

Her lips pressed together, and the groundswell of loneliness pushed into her chest. Boundaries and alliances had been formed, and she was on the outside. Her flat was an empty echo of her life.

"When did it become this way, Sarah?" she addressed the woman in the mural. Sarah's painted lips remained in the same soft curve. Freya went over to the wall and placed her fingertips on the heart and throat chakras of Sarah's image. She closed her eyes and focused on her fingertips, willing a connection. But there was no comfort from the painted figure. She dropped her hand and turned away. Her fingertips throbbed, but not from the touch on the wall, but with the memory of warm flesh. *Lily.*

Without waiting for the kettle, she fed Dorcas and went down to the shop early. She had stock to unpack. Maybe she could try a new window display.

There was no yoga the next morning. Freya sat on her balcony with a cup of hot water and lemon, Dorcas on her knee. A soft thud sounded, and a grey-and-white cat leapt down from the rail and approached. It was small, tiny really. Dorcas watched the newcomer and let out a soft meow, welcome or protest Freya couldn't tell. The little kitty climbed onto the couch next to Freya, and put tentative paws on her leg.

"Well, hello." She rubbed the cat's head and smiled as it arched up in expectation of more.

The cat jumped down and stalked off, tail quivering, to explore inside Freya's apartment.

"Mabel... Where are you?" Lily's voice sounded through the wall.

Then Carly's. "She can't be far. Maybe she's hiding under furniture." There was the thump of something being dragged. "Nope, not under the bed. That's where she was last time."

Lily's voice came closer. "Carly, the balcony door is open. She must have got out."

Carly's tones were worried as she replied, "She's never been out there before. What if she's fallen over the rail?"

"She's a *cat*. They always land right-side up."

"But she's so little."

Freya looked at the cat, now on her counter sniffing the teabags. She scooped her up and the little cat settled into her arms and started purring. With Mabel clinging to her T-shirt, she went out to the balcony. "Lily?"

There was no answer. Lily and Carly were talking inside the flat.

She thought about putting Mabel back on Lily's side of the balcony and trusting she'd find her own way back. But what if she did fall or escape? With a sigh, she headed downstairs to Lily's door and rang the bell. There was a clatter on the stairs and the door was flung open. Carly stood there.

"You've found her! Oh, the poor little darling." She reached out and took Mabel. "Come in, Frey. Lily will be delighted. We hadn't seen her since last night. Where was she?"

"She appeared on my side of the balcony this morning."

"Come on up." Carly turned away, the cat in her arms.

"Thanks, but I need to keep moving."

Carly paused on the stairs and turned around to face her. "Oh, that's a shame. Not even time for a cuppa?"

"No." Freya hesitated, then the words came in a rush. "Where were you yesterday? I didn't know you weren't coming to yoga."

Carly's glance strayed up the stairs, and then she came back down. "I couldn't face it. All the people. I know everyone means well, but I keep seeing the sympathy in their eyes. I'm sorry, Frey, I should have called to let you know."

"Is everything okay?" She kept her eyes firmly on Mabel, now clinging to Carly's bosom.

Carly dropped her face to snuggle into Mabel's fur. "No. Not really. Andy's being a total dick. He changed the locks on the house so I can't get in. I used to go when he wasn't there, get more clothes, pantry items, small things like books."

Freya frowned. "He can't do that."

"You don't need to tell me. But he has."

"Would you like me to come with you to demand a key?"

"I don't know what I want, to be honest. I stayed here the last few nights. My new flat just seemed so unwelcoming, I didn't want to be there."

That selfish pang again, the one that was slighted that Carly had gone to Lily, instead of her. She should be happy Carly had friends she could stay with.

"You're welcome to stay with me anytime." She found Carly's fingers where they clutched Mabel to her chest and gave a gentle squeeze.

"I know. Thank you."

Mabel wiggled and flexed her claws against Carly's T-shirt. Carly yelped. "I better take our escape artist home before she makes another break for it." She kissed Freya on the cheek and then took the stairs two at a time, the wriggling cat in her arms.

Freya pulled the door closed and turned away to her own door.

She thought about texting Carly to see if she was coming to yoga the next morning, but she put her mobile down, the text unsent. Carly was a big girl; she didn't need the reminder. But the next morning, the class was emptier without Lily's presence, and Carly too was missing.

She sent her a text when yoga was over: *breakfast?*

There was no immediate reply. She tidied the yoga room. Lily's class was the next scheduled use, and so, on an impulse, she arranged the room in the configuration Lily used. This would be the first class since she'd left so precipitously. Freya sat heavily in one of the beanbags. This would be where she'd sit if she went. Lily would be at the front of the room, a compelling, positive figure.

Freya hadn't thought about the class since she'd fled. Every time she saw the crumpled sheets of her writing on her kitchen counter, her gaze flitted away. She couldn't bring herself to read what she'd written. She should. The anger and haze of that time was a blur in her mind and she had no idea—none—as to what she'd find on the page. The memories in her head were of Lily taunting her, of her hand moving over the white page until it was covered in her neat, tight writing. The feeling that had generated was one of relief. It was out. Out in the air, in the world, committed to paper. As the words flowed, moment by moment the pain and tightness left her chest. It was about Sarah, that much she remembered, about love and loss and letting go. But the specifics of the words, what they would mean to her life going forwards—they eluded her. Only their vibration in her heart remained.

Lily had done that. Encouraged, cajoled, goaded until the dam wall burst. Freya should attend the class; it would be the honourable thing to do. A recognition of her transformation.

But she hadn't seen Lily since.

She clenched her fist on her knee. How dare she? How dare Lily shove her out onto the open ground, her feelings raw and exposed and new and then abandon her? Ignore her?

Her phone vibrated with a text message, but it wasn't Carly. It was, of all people, Janie wondering if she felt like meeting for lunch.

Janie? The spurt of anger surged again. Had Lily directed her unwanted would-be partner to try her luck with Freya again?

She left the message unanswered and went through her shop to the shared entrance. She'd paused at her door to turn her sign to *Welcome, Friend* when the voices made her hesitate. Carly and Lily.

Freya waited, her hand on the sign. Their voices reached her clearly.

"Thanks, darling." The warmth in Carly's voice made her pause. There was an intimacy in her tone, a caressing quality. Freya peered through the glass door.

Carly was half turned away from her, and she leant forwards and kissed Lily on the cheek. It wasn't a swift peck; it lingered. It implied warmth and intimacy, a closeness of friendship.

"Thanks," she said again. "See you later."

Freya retreated, a step back into her dimly lit shop, unwilling to be seen.

Lily glanced around the room. Freya wasn't there. The surprise would have been if she had come, after the previous week. The memory of glittering eyes glaring in accusation and pain still haunted her, stealing into her mind in quiet moments.

She shouldn't have needled Freya. She had pushed too hard. She should have let Freya find her own way out of her self-imposed boundaries in her own time. It was arrogant and presumptuous of her to think she could bust down those walls and allow Freya to step forth again.

Lily focused on Janie in the front row. "Last week, we used writing as a method of expression. Today, we're going to use our voices. As before, no one has to do anything they are not comfortable with. But vocalising that which holds us back is another way to let it go. No one will hear what you say unless you want them to. Sing, hum, shout, or whisper. Your choice."

She looked around at the rapt faces in front of her. She was doing a good thing with this class, of that she was sure. But for herself, things weren't as good. She hadn't been to yoga for nearly a week—she couldn't face the scorn in Freya's eyes.

The words she should express herself hovered on her lips. Whether she had the courage to say them... She pushed people to change. She sought to give them courage to face things no one would ever choose for themselves. Courage to change things. It was all very well for her to push Freya to change, but Freya had to want it.

And, she acknowledged, part of the reason she was pushing for that change was in the hope that Freya would see Lily as more than an irritating neighbour. That she would reflect on the kisses they had shared and crave more. That Freya would choose a life with Lily.

Freya was lodged firmly under Lily's skin. She was behind her eyelids during meditation, the last thing Lily thought of when she went to sleep, and even then, there was no respite, for Freya paraded through her dreams. A dream Freya; one who laughed and loved, whose scorn was missing, and whose silver eyes were soft and misty with desire.

She had fallen silent during her contemplation. Let the class think it was the inwards reflection needed for the exercise.

"Spread out," she instructed. "Find the words in your own time."

The need to express herself in the same way was overwhelming. She found a quiet space in the middle of the room so the corners could be saved for the timid who needed the security of walls. Lily sat in lotus pose, her hands on her knees, palms open to the ceiling.

A few deep breaths, an inwards focus, drawing her energy to where she needed it. She let the thought coalesce, into a coil of a whisper in her chest. *Freya.* She would whisper her need, her want, her desire to the warm air of the room. No one would hear; the privacy and open space of the yoga room would see to that. Dimly, around her, she heard murmurs and whispers, too distant, too quiet, to hear.

Lily focused on the word. *Freya.* The words around that name would find themselves when she vocalised them. One more deep breath to steady herself, and then she spoke.

What came out was a shout, a paean, a belly laugh that started at her toes and travelled through her body before it erupted from her mouth.

I love Freya.

Had she really said that? The silence in the room was her answer. She scrunched her eyes tight; the stunned faces of her class were already there in her imagination. She didn't need to see them. Gradually, the murmur of voices restarted.

Her heart beat a frantic pulse in her chest. Lily concentrated on her breath rather than spiral into the dismay of discovery. After all, this was exactly what this workshop was about. Discovery, self-discovery. These women would not give away her secret.

More minutes passed before she called a halt to the session. She smiled around at the women, pushing aside her own discomfort to focus on them. "Does anyone want to talk?"

Carly followed her up to the flat after the class and perched on one of the stools at the breakfast bar. "Are you still okay with me being here?" she asked. "I didn't expect to be here this long."

"It's fine with me." Lily poured them both a glass of water. "Stay as long as you want."

"Thanks. I should try staying over at the flat again. I will. Maybe tomorrow." Carly stared down at the counter, drawing a pattern with a finger.

Lily rummaged in the fridge, pulling out cauliflower, soy cheese, and mushrooms. That would turn into comfort food. It looked like Carly needed it. And red wine. She found a bottle tucked in the back of the pantry. When she turned, Carly was searching in the kitchen drawer for cutlery.

"I'm not so selfish that I have to talk about me all the time." Carly directed the words to the teaspoons. "We can pretend I didn't hear what you shouted in class earlier. Or we can talk about it."

"What's said in class, stays in class." Lily twisted the screw top on the wine with unnecessary force.

"Is that a no?"

"It's a no."

"You and Freya are equally stubborn. You deserve each other." Carly set the cutlery on the counter and for the first time since the night at the bar a smile lit her face. "I won't tell her."

Chapter 18

"WHAT THE FUCK ARE YOU doing with my wife!"

Lily blinked awake, disorientated, but springing into overdrive. Her flat, her bedroom, but very definitely not her man standing by the bed, face beetroot, and hands balled into fists. Beside her, Carly stirred, pushing herself up on her hands. "Andy! What are you doing here? How did you get in?"

"Is that all you can say? I catch you in bed with your lesbo girlfriend, and all you wonder is how I got in?"

"Lily isn't my—"

The mist of confusion parted in Lily's head. "The question of how you got in *is* important. Breaking and entering."

"The door wasn't locked."

Lily grabbed her mobile from the bedside table, got out of bed, and stood tall facing Andy. She pushed her hair back from her face, willing her fingers to remain steady. Despite the knowledge she was in the right, her position was a vulnerable one. A T-shirt and undies, however long and baggy the T-shirt, made her feel exposed. "Leave. Now. You're not welcome here."

"You're in bed with my wife!"

Lily ignored that. She daren't look at Carly to see how her friend was taking the confrontation. "If you don't leave now, I'm calling the police."

"Carls won't let you. Will you, Carls?"

"It's nothing to do with Carly. This is my property. This is a home invasion and is therefore a police matter." She closed her fingers tightly around the mobile in her hand.

"She's my fucking *wife*. You don't have the right." Andy took a pace towards her.

Carly scrambled out of bed. "Andy, stop it. Get out of here and go home."

"Not without my wife!"

"That would be the wife you threw over for a younger model with better bodywork without a second thought? The wife whom you thought would be content to remain at home eating toast and vegemite to save money for IVF whilst you took your girlfriend to the fancy restaurant you told me we couldn't afford? That would be the wife whom you only seemed to notice when she was *not* at home? That wife? Is that the one you mean?" Carly's voice rose from a quiet growl to a shout as she gained in strength. "Listen to me, Andy, and listen good. I am not your possession. I thought I was your equal, your mate, your partner. You've shown me I was wrong. And if Lily won't call the police, I will."

"The fuck you will. They'll side with me."

Lily turned away to shield her actions and punched out Triple Zero with shaking fingers.

"Emergency assistance. Do you need police, fire and rescue, or ambulance?"

"Police."

Andy moved forwards and backhanded the phone from Lily's hand. It flew across the room and hit the wall with a dull thud. A glance at the screen showed the call had disconnected.

She didn't let herself flinch when Andy came towards her again, but he kept on going until he could grab Carly by the wrist. "We're leaving."

"We're not." Carly jerked back but couldn't break free.

Andy's feral grin sickened Lily. "Let her go." She put as much authority in her voice as she could muster.

"Make me." Andy twisted Carly's arm up behind her, forcing her to sink down to relieve the tension on her shoulder.

There was nothing in the room that would make an effective weapon. No heavy ornaments, no water glass on the bedside table. Even her shoes were rubber thongs. Lily lowered her head and charged Andy like a bull. Her head thudded into his abdomen, sending a sharp wave of pain down her neck. She ignored it. Andy grunted, and his arm came down with heavy force across her shoulders.

"Bitch." His backhander caught the side of her face, and pain bloomed over her cheek.

She backed away before he could grab her.

With a sharp movement, Andy twisted Carly's arm up further behind her back. "We're going."

"You're not." The voice in the doorway was cold, hard like tempered steel, cutting like glass. "The police are on their way. I'd say less than five minutes, given how close the cop shop is." Freya advanced into the room. Her mobile was in one hand, the Active Call light blinking. She held one of the wrought-iron pokers from her shop, and she threw the matching ember shovel to Lily. The twisted metal was cool and solid in her hand.

"Now would be a good time to let Carly go." Freya's tone was conversational; she could have been making small talk at a party. "Probably best to do it before the police arrive. They take a hard line on hostage situations."

"Carls isn't a hostage. She's coming with me willingly." Andy jerked her arm again, his grip tightening on her wrist.

"Let me go!" Carly kicked backwards with her bare foot striking his shin.

He laughed. "Try harder, darling. But you always did like it rough, didn't you?"

"Let me *go*." Carly's voice trembled.

Freya lifted the poker and wielded it like a cricket bat. Lily copied her movement on Andy's other side. Freya's presence had sharpened her mind. Her shoulders and neck screamed in pain, but she pushed that away.

"What are you going to do? Tap me with that little matchstick?" Andy shoved Carly towards the door.

Freya swung. The poker came down in the perfect arc of a golf swing that connected at the backs of Andy's legs. He lurched, his knees buckling, and his grip loosened. With a twist, Carly broke free.

"Get out," Freya hissed to her. "Lily and I will keep him here until the police come. Go out to the street and flag them down."

With a panicked cry, Carly fled, her bare feet making soft noises on the wooden floor.

Andy had barely straightened when Freya swung again. This time her aim was better and the poker slammed right into the crease behind his knees. He staggered around and lunged for her, but she dodged, flitting out of the way.

Lily swallowed, her heart in her throat as Andy switched his gaze to her. The menace in it chilled her to the core.

"I'd rather get you, the one who corrupted my wife."

The automatic denial rose in her throat, but she swallowed the words. It was pointless. She inched away. "Carly's my friend. I want what's best for her."

Out of the corner of her eye, she saw Freya's grip tighten on the poker. Lily grasped her own weapon and held it in front of her with two hands.

"You've been poisoning her mind since you met her." Andy's gaze switched to Freya. "You too, but you were always the harmless one."

Freya seemed anything but harmless now. She was ice and balm to Lily's barely contained fear, strength radiating from her in supportive waves.

"You always underestimate people, Andy." Freya circled around and watched like a cat as Andy turned a smaller circle to keep her in sight.

His back was to Lily. She didn't stop to analyse the move, the sense of it, its possible effectiveness. She acted on instinct and swung her shovel as hard as she could, copying Freya's swing. The shock of it connecting against the backs of Andy's legs sent reverberations up her arms into her sore shoulders. Andy staggered, and whilst he was momentarily off balance, Lily dropped the shovel and charged. Her bulk caught him in the lower back, and he fell forwards, face down on the bed.

Lily dropped on top of him, her knees jamming into his lower back. Freya followed, yanking his arms above his head.

"Bedside drawer," Lily grunted as Andy thrashed beneath her. "Handcuffs."

Freya lunged for the drawer with one hand and withdrew the handcuffs. Pink and fur-lined, they were a sexy toy designed for play rather than real restraint, but they would suffice for a few minutes until the police came. Freya fumbled, turning the cuffs over in her hands until she found the catch. His hands free, Andy thrashed, his arms flailing. The cuffs sprung open, and Freya snatched one of Andy's hands and jammed the cuff around his wrist. Designed for a smaller frame than his, it was hard to close. The click as it snicked shut was the sweetest sound Lily had heard in a long time.

Andy tried to free himself, but Freya's wiry frame had a supple strength, and with one yank, she got his arm closer to the metal bed frame. A second click, and he was secured to the frame by one wrist.

Lily leapt away. It was a poor fix; Andy still had one hand free. Freya moved to stand next to her, close enough that their hands brushed. Lily's fingers trembled, and maybe sensing this, Freya reached down and clasped them in her warm hand. Steadiness and reassurance flowed through her grasp.

Thundering feet came up the stairs, and then two police officers entered.

"You fucking bitch." Andy tried to roll over. "It's not what it seems, officer. Just a little game that went a bit far."

The policewoman's gaze went from the pink fur-lined handcuffs, and swept over Freya and Lily, still hand in hand, back to where Carly hovered in the doorway. Her gaze hardened and went back to Andy. "You're under arrest." She turned to her colleague. "Cuff him. Again."

Andy was quiet as the male officer cuffed him securely.

The female turned to Carly. "Are you okay? Do you need a doctor?"

Carly shook her head. "He didn't hurt me much. Just grabbed my arm. Do I have to come to the station too?"

The officer's gaze softened. "Are you up to it? All three of you?"

Freya nodded. Lily glanced around her bedroom. All she wanted was to set the room to rights, change the sheets, crawl into bed, and sleep. Later. That would be later. First, she had to give a statement and then make sure Carly was okay.

Dawn was breaking as the three of them left the police station. The chorus of birdsong swelled around them as they walked away. Without debate, they went back to the shops, through the quiet streets softly lit by the dawn light.

Freya stifled a yawn, and reached out to grasp Carly's hand. "Tell me what I can do, Carly."

"Can I come home with you?" Carly's voice was small. "I'm sorry, Lily, but I can't face your flat right now."

"Understandable. I'm not sure I want to be there either."

They reached the doors where A Woman's Pleasure and A Woman's Spirit faced each other across the tiled alcove. Freya led the way into her shop.

"I need to check on Mabel." Lily's dark skin seemed sallow in the morning light. Her hair was in a messy ponytail, and although she and Carly had dressed before going down the police station, Lily still had a subdued, dishevelled look.

Freya nodded. "Come up when you're ready."

Once in Freya's living area, Carly flung herself on the couch, her hand over her eyes. "This isn't how it was supposed to be."

Freya perched on the couch at Carly's head and lifted Carly's clenched fist from her eyes. "Life isn't a certainty. I wish it was. I wish we knew how things would turn out."

"I never thought it would be like this. My life. It was supposed to be domestic bliss and happiness. Kids. Life in a small town that I love. My husband wasn't supposed to turn into an unfaithful bully."

Freya was silent. Whole scenarios ran through her head: of relationships, nascent and nurturing, flowing, developing. Dead or dying. Carly had always seemed content in her marriage. Her lips twisted wryly. She obviously didn't know her friend as well as she'd thought. She'd taken Carly's whinges to be the usual grumbles of any relationship. And Carly's upbeat personality had made it easy for her to skate over the deeper dissatisfactions.

She stroked Carly's hair, cupped her cheek in a tender gesture.

"I don't know how I'll cope alone." Carly's eyes had the sheen of unshed tears. "Look at me. I can't even go home to my flat. I've been staying with Lily as I didn't want to be alone. Now I'm staying with you."

"We're here for you. Both of us. Stay as long as you want."

"Lily's been fantastic. Supportive and comforting. I'm pathetic." A tear ran down her cheek, but she didn't seem to notice. "I can't even sleep on my own. I need to know someone's close by. It's false security, though. When it came to it, Andy just waltzed right into Lily's bedroom. Lily was great. And you…"

"I heard the crash through the wall. They're thin. I heard the shouting, the words."

"Thank you." Carly captured Freya's hand and held it between hers. "Many people would have rolled over and gone back to sleep, or banged on the wall and shouted to keep the noise down."

Footsteps sounded on the stairs and Lily reappeared, Mabel in her arms. "I hope you don't mind. She must have been very scared. It took me a bit to find her; she was hiding in the laundry basket."

"That's fine." Freya watched as the cat stalked off and found Dorcas, where she was sprawled on the couch. "Does anyone want coffee?"

"Love some." Carly's eyes had dark rings under them, and her face was pinched and drawn, but she managed a smile. "I'll make it." She disappeared in the direction of the kitchen, and there was the sound of cupboards opening and closing, and a tap running.

Left alone with Lily, Freya found she didn't know what to say.

Lily seemed far away. Freya followed her gaze over to the mural. The curling lushness of an Australian rainforest. The two naked women, hand in hand, like Eves of a happier time. But instead of studying the art of the finished part, Lily was studying the unfinished section, where the paint ran into a pencilled outline, and then into nothing but white wall.

Lily's mouth turned down in a rueful twist and she went over to sit next to Mabel, and petted the small head in soothing strokes. "You can talk to me." Her head bent as her fingers passed over the cat's fur. "Andy was way wrong. Carly was in my bed purely because she was nervous and didn't want to be alone. No other reason." She shot a glance towards the kitchen. "I honestly don't know how she'll go alone. She'll need our support, I think."

"I know."

"Know?" Lily's brow furrowed and she shot a quizzical glance in Freya's direction. "About... Oh!" Suddenly, she was seriousness personified. She picked up Mabel and moved over to where Freya still sat at the table.

She held out a hand, and Freya took it. Lily's fingers were warm in her own suddenly chilled ones. She stood, face-to-face with her neighbour.

"You thought Carly and I were lovers." Amusement lit her face from within. "Freya, *honestly*." The amused tenderness in her voice made Freya's knees shake. Mabel squirmed for release, and Lily set her on the floor. When she straightened again, she was closer. Near enough to tuck one of Freya's wiry curls behind her ear, near enough to trail a finger over Freya's cheek, along the edge of cheekbone to rest on her lips. "Freya, you are so wrong. There's only one person in my head. One person who steals my thoughts, controls my heartbeat."

The words were locked in Freya's throat. Lily wanted *her*. Oh, she'd intimated that before, played with the idea, but it had always seemed like a passing fancy, that Freya was just another in the line of playthings, sexual playmates, in a revolving door to Lily's bed. Nothing serious. Nothing lasting.

Not like Sarah.

Lily's finger ran across Freya's bottom lip, slowly, a millimetre at a time, lighting the nerve endings in its wake. Freya's core melted. Boneless; she was boneless, a molten waxen thing, tilting in Lily's direction.

Lily's finger dropped away and she took a step back. Freya swayed, disoriented by the abrupt withdrawal.

"Coffee." Carly's voice was bright with artificial bonhomie as she set two mugs on the table. "I still can't find your sugar, Frey. I swear you hide it from me deliberately."

"I do." Was that her voice, so normal, so steady? "It's at the very back of the cupboard over the sink, behind the lentils."

Carly disappeared back to the kitchen.

"I'm not letting you run away from me again, Freya." Lily's voice was soft. "We can move as slow as you like, but we will move forwards. One day, I hope we can be girlfriends. Partners maybe, if we are lucky. Do you think that is something you can try for?"

"Yes." Freya spoke the word without hesitation. It was right. It was time. "Lily, I'm sorry. For so many things: making it difficult for you when you first arrived, about the workshop space. For not being as welcoming as I should have been. I—"

"Shush." Lily looked at their cats, now curled around each other on the couch. "I was difficult with you too." She glanced towards the kitchen. "Let's see what we can do to help Carly before we try and entwine our own lives."

Chapter 19

THE NEXT COUPLE OF WEEKS passed in a blur of events. Andy was charged with a string of offences involving his entry into Lily's flat, including threatening behaviour and property damage. He was released on bail and vanished to Mackay. Freya bumped into him at the supermarket with a trolley full of expensive brands. Kim was by his side.

"Good riddance," Carly said when she heard that piece of news, and promptly put her head on her folded arms on the table and burst into tears.

She had the support of friends. Remy took her to Mackay and helped her choose furniture; Janie, who was quite a whiz with decor, took her shopping for curtains and rugs; and other friends dropped around with small items, unwanted things, they said, that would be oh so perfect for Carly's new flat.

Carly stayed with Freya for ten days and then moved back to her flat. For a few days, either Lily or Freya stayed overnight with her, and then Carly decided enough was enough and said she was ready to stay alone.

Lily, who'd come prepared for an overnight visit, kissed her cheek and went home. After the ruckus of the previous couple of weeks, her flat seemed eerily quiet. Its warm timber floor absorbed the soft footfalls her bare feet made as she moved softly around, feeding Mabel and pouring a glass of water before sinking onto the couch on the balcony.

It was a Sunday. There was yoga in the morning, a class where she would take her usual position at the back of the room and let her body relax into the slow movements and poses and quiet space that was one of Freya's classes. Her shop didn't open on Mondays. It was her day to herself—if errands and housework counted as quality time alone. Mabel played at her feet, entertaining herself by batting one of the cushion tassels around with velvet paws.

Lily looked back into her flat. There were still small traces of Carly in the space, even though she hadn't stayed over for a while. A tube of mascara sat on the counter. The brand of muesli she liked sagged on the kitchen table, and Mabel had found a shiny earring to play with. The flat felt empty without Carly. Lily had lived with Inga for nearly four years, and less than a year by herself since then. She'd often been alone, but never lonely. Now the flat had a quietness about it that was less peace and more lonesome. She picked up Mabel and smiled as the cat turned around and settled on her lap. The joy in her own space would return.

The doorbell rang and for a moment she considered not answering. But only for a moment, because the tingle of nerve endings made her think of Freya. With Mabel cradled in one arm, she swung open the door. Freya stood there.

"It was open. You could have just come up."

"I didn't want to bring up bad memories." Thoughtful Freya.

"Andy has no place in my headspace, and certainly not in my home. If the door's open, feel free to come up anytime."

"Thank you."

Now that Freya was in her space, Lily didn't know where to start. Freya, too, seemed lost for words.

"Water? Tea?"

"Tea, please." Freya followed her into the kitchen. "Carly rang. She said to tell you she's fine. She told me she was now ready to go it alone in her flat."

"I think she'll be all right. It will be hard, though."

"She has good friends. You."

"And you." Lily busied herself with teabags and boiling water. "She'll be okay."

The space between them had never seemed wider. Lily pulled the teabag out of her mug, left it on the saucer, fiddled with the tag. She pushed a mug over to Freya.

"I don't know what to say to you." Freya's quiet words cut through the silence that sat between them. "This is our time to move forwards, a time for a beginning, but I don't know where to start."

The words, so tentative, so unsure, so un-Freya, settled Lily. They both could do this. "Will you go out with me, Freya? Tonight, maybe?"

"Out?"

"Yes. We've spent so much time within these walls: your flat, mine. Your shop, the workshop. We haven't been many places together."

"Breakfast, at the Green House."

"Yes. With Carly, and with Remy looking on. I'd like to take you to dinner, just the two of us. Not in Grasstree Flat. There's a little harbourside restaurant along the coast. Very informal. They always have a couple of vegan dishes on the menu. Will you come?"

She waited, heart pounding for Freya's answer.

Freya nodded, a barely discernible up and down. "I'd like that."

"Can you be ready by five? If so, we could walk on the beach first."

Freya's smile flickered over her face, as shifting as the moonglade. "That's what people on a date do."

Lily's smile lit her eyes. "Exactly."

There was a knock on her door just before five. Lily stood there, wearing a diagonally printed top over a maxi skirt. Her dark hair hung smoothly to below her shoulders, and her arms glowed bronze underneath the yellow light in the porch. Freya was caught in the moment, her feet glued to the floor, unable to tear her gaze from Lily.

Her heartbeat slowed from the fast patter that had consumed her since she had agreed to go on a date with Lily. It would be all right.

Lily held out a hand and Freya took it, her fingers clasping Lily's.

Close up, Lily's pupils were wide in her warm brown eyes. Her lips parted into a slow smile. "You look beautiful."

Freya picked at her loose Indian pants. "No. But thank you."

Lily lifted their joined hands. "Don't argue. It's my eyes that are seeing you."

The touch of her hand and the heat of her gaze warmed Freya equally. She stepped out in the shared entranceway between their shops. A Woman's Pleasure was in darkness, only the blink of a blue security light above the door. Freya pulled her door closed with her free hand.

Lily drove her bright yellow hatchback as jauntily as the colour implied. The road to the coast was quiet, and the little car hugged the tight bends on the narrow road. Lily drove with skill, her hands sure on the wheel, using the gears like a pro. She didn't seem inclined to talk, and Freya appreciated the silence. Words she should say bubbled inside her chest, but the time and place wasn't this too-small car on a twisting road. There would be time over dinner.

Lily passed the turn to Mackay and continued south on the highway for another few minutes before turning down an unmarked gravel road that meandered through fields of sugar cane and pineapples to end abruptly at a boat ramp. Mangroves stretched north along the coast, but to the south a white sandy beach curved for a kilometre or so. The water was the clear blue of the Coral Sea. Lily parked the car beside the sign warning of saltwater crocodiles, and the two of them walked down to the sand.

A lone fisherman winched his boat up onto the trailer behind his four-wheel drive, but apart from him, the spot was deserted. Lily slipped off her sandals and left them at the edge of the gravel. Freya followed suit and they meandered down the beach to the water's edge. The tide was low, and their feet sank into the glistening expanse of sand. There was no surf this far north; the offshore Great Barrier Reef took the curl from the water, leaving it smooth and glassy, with only the tiniest of wavelets lapping to shore.

Freya bent to pick up the empty fan of a pipi shell and cupped it in her hand. Such shells were scattered over the beach, but she studied the whorls and ridges as if they were new to her.

It was easier than looking at Lily, standing a pace away. She ran a fingertip over the sharp edge. It was brittle and caught on her skin. Lily moved closer and her hands came out to clasp Freya's, stilling their motion.

"Leave it," she said. "Let's walk." With great care, she prised Freya's fingers open, one by one, until the shell dropped to the sand.

She threaded her fingers through Freya's and clasped tight. When she moved away, down the beach to where the palm trees leant over the sand, Freya was tugged along by their link.

Their path led them through the warm shallow waters that ran into the shore. Tiny crabs scuttled away in front of them, and fish darted away into deeper water. At the end of the bay, where a pile of granite boulders blocked the way, Lily stopped.

Her eyes crinkled as she said, "Shall we head back? I'm looking forwards to dinner."

Freya turned to face the sea. Words she wanted to say bubbled up inside her, like a waterspout. Her toes curled into the sand. "There's things I need to tell you. About Sarah. About me and Sarah."

Lily's smile slipped from her face and she raised their linked hands. "And I would like to hear them. Is now the time?"

"I think so." Freya turned to head back along the beach. Their linked hands still swung between them, and the water was tepid around her ankles. She bent to roll up the cuffs of her pants a little higher. "Sarah and I were together for seven years. That's not long in the scheme of things. My parents are still together after fifty. So maybe if Sarah had lived, we would still be happy together, maybe not. I think it would be the former. We had so much happiness, and we had so much love. We made love often." She smiled slightly. "No lesbian bed death in our home. It was an important, joyous part of our relationship.

"Her breast cancer diagnosis came out of the blue. I've already told you it was a late diagnosis and an aggressive tumour. There were already secondaries in her lungs and bones. She had radiotherapy, and she had one course of chemo. It was an attempt at staving off the inevitable and she didn't react well to the treatment at all. She was miserable, tired, sick. She kept saying what was the point, and that she didn't want me to remember her like this. She made the decision that she would cease treatment and face the future on her own terms. For her, it was the right decision. I'm not saying it should be that way for everyone, but although she only had a few months left, she regained her happiness, her serene nature, and her joy in living."

Freya fell silent. Memories washed over her. Sarah's face when she told her she was ceasing treatment, her stoic suffering. Her grip on Freya's hand as she lay in the hospice, her breathing the erratic pattern that precedes death. Freya swallowed. Time had painted these memories with a patina of distance, but picking away at that covering left them raw again.

Lily was silent beside her, but her hand clasp was steady, unwavering.

"Sarah turned to alternate therapies. I don't think they made a difference; things had progressed to the point where little would have helped, but it gave her back control of her life, and that was important." She heaved a breath. "And Sarah stopped making love. Part of it was a lessening of desire as her body was so sick. But a large part of it was a belief that she had to rise above the physical. Prepare for her life to come, if you like. The next life. She wasn't religious, but she was spiritual.

She believed there was some greater plane after death, even if she didn't know what or where or how. She started to read spiritual texts, some religious ones. Even things like quantum physics." Freya smiled, remembering. "She used to joke that her body was dead or alive depending on who was looking at it. Her seeking of the spiritual led her to repudiate the physical." Dimly, she was aware that she had halted, up to her ankles in the salty water. Lily stopped too, their fingers still tightly entwined.

"She was still affectionate. I knew she still loved me. We still cuddled, kissed, slept spooned together at night, still held hands as we took the gentle walks along the river that were all she could manage. But we never again made love."

Freya dragged a deep breath and collected her thoughts, which were scattering away from her on the sea breeze. "I didn't take it well at first. She was still my partner; I loved her in every way and that included lovemaking. I didn't see why a spiritual path should preclude a physical one, especially not in the loving relationship we shared. But Sarah refused to consider the idea. She said, quite rightly, that it was her life, her body, and although she loved me as much as ever, she needed to focus her mind on the journey ahead. And she couldn't do that if her energy and direction were dissipated by lovemaking."

"What did you do?" Lily's words were quiet, but they scythed through the turbulence in Freya's mind.

"I begged. I said she may not need lovemaking anymore, but that I did, and I wanted—needed—that reaffirmation of our love. Sarah said she was sorry, so very sorry, but she had to put herself first and she truly believed her chosen path was the right one for her.

"I got a little desperate. I thought maybe she was insecure about her body. She was emaciated and her hair was thin. I didn't care about her looks; they were never important. She was my Sarah and I loved her. But she was adamant. Deep down, I respected and acknowledged her right to do what she felt was right for her, but a part of me hated that she didn't love me enough to make love with me one more time. A last time, to give me something to cling to. But it was, after all, her body and her choice."

"What happened?" Lily raised their linked fingers and pressed the back of Freya's hand to her lips. A soft touch, then their joined hands swung between them once more.

"I gave her an ultimatum. I said if she didn't at least let me make love to her once more, I would leave as I couldn't face seeing her die without something sweet I could cling to." Tears glistened in Freya's eyes. "The minute the words left my mouth, I knew I'd done something so hateful that I could never make it up or take it back. I'd demanded something she was not prepared to give, and which she had every right to withhold. We were in bed at the time. I was spooning her, big spoon to her little spoon, and I clasped her hand over her remaining breast. She was silent for a moment. Then she turned her head and spoke over her shoulder. 'I can't, Freya. And if that's the cost, then I will pay the price.' She moved away from me, and left me lying there, feeling so unutterably wretched. Miserable that I'd asked something of her she couldn't give, hating myself for putting a condition on my love. I hadn't meant it, of course. I would never have left her. I didn't want to. I wanted to take every word, every breath, every kiss, every moment I could spend with her while I could.

"I apologised. I abased myself. I cried. I told her over and over how much I loved her and that I would never leave. She turned to me, kissed me once softly on the forehead, and told me that she knew, that she loved me as deeply and she was truly sorry she couldn't give me what I needed. We cried ourselves to sleep."

Freya's words petered out. Her gaze followed a pelican as it came in to land on the water. "She died seventeen days later."

Lily released Freya's hand and stepped forwards. She gathered Freya against her bosom, holding her cradled against her warmth. One hand stroked Freya's hair, the other curved around her shoulders as they trembled with the silent tears flowing down her face.

Freya pressed her face to Lily's breasts, taking the wordless comfort offered. Images of Sarah filled her mind: dancing at their commitment ceremony, laughing at a bad joke, serene in a meditation class, smiling with her face up to the sun as she strolled along the river.

"I loved her so much." Her voice was muffled by Lily's body. "And I felt so guilty. When she died, when the grief was so consuming I didn't know how I'd get through the next few minutes, let alone the days or weeks to come, I started reading her books. There was a pile of them, spiritual books mainly, her quest for knowledge of what would come next for her. I read them to be closer to her, to understand what she went though. Then, I found her diary. It was tucked away in the back of her underwear drawer. As well as being an outpouring of her love for me, I learnt of her inner journey.

"I started along her path as a way of remaining close to her. If I could feel what she felt, maybe I could reach her spirit. At the least, I would be closer to her and she would remain in my head." She raised her head from Lily's breast. "And until recently, I have never wavered from that path."

Lily's hand stroked Freya's hair, a soothing motion that lingered at the end of each stroke.

"And now?" The words were quiet, spoken to the warm air above Freya's head. "Do you still want that path?"

"It's a part of me now. A more spiritual way of life. Accepting there are some things we can never understand, at least not until we, too, move to the next stage of our spirit journeys. But I'm grounded on earth, this town that I love. And Sarah's path was right for her at that time in her life, but it's not right for me, not now. Not anymore." Her smile was tremulous. "Parts of what I learnt will never leave, but it's time for me to try and get back all of my life. Relearn what I loved so long ago."

"Love." The word was a susurration of breath.

"Yes, love. Here in the present. In all its myriad of expression. Including physical, sexual love. Will you help me regain that part of myself, Lily?"

Lily grasped her shoulders and stepped back a pace. Her gaze swept over Freya from head to toe and Freya shivered in its intensity. "There is nothing I would like more. Nothing."

Freya wasn't sure who moved first, but they came together in a long embrace, arms seeking and finding their way around each other's backs, to hold the other close. The setting sun was warm on Freya's shoulders as she raised her arms to draw Lily closer.

There was so much comfort in Lily's embrace, so much wordless understanding. Freya rested her head on Lily's shoulder. Lily radiated calm. Freya was glad Lily hadn't overridden her spilling of the past in a welter of words. Lily's gentle prompts had been enough. There would be questions later, she was sure, but for now, Lily's quiet acceptance that, yes, that was how it had been for Freya, that had been Freya's experience, was the response she needed. In the past, when well-meaning friends had tried to get her to talk about Sarah and Freya's own direction in life, it had been with incomprehension, with an unspoken wish to get Freya *back to normal*. Whatever that was. But now, the sunlight seeping into the corners of her mind and the tingles pulsing in her fingertips reaffirmed her joy in life. Sarah was still a part of her, but now Lily was too.

Lily released her clasp long enough to tuck a stray curl behind Freya's ear, and smiled when it immediately sprung free.

"That's you," she said. "So much life and energy. I'm glad you're letting it loose again." She bent her head and took Freya's lips in a kiss that was warm and salty and damp and lingered for long moments. Her breath was warm in Freya's mouth, her lips mobile as they touched and released before she moved apart.

"I like being able to do that." She turned to face where the little yellow car sat facing the sea. "But maybe we should go for dinner."

Chapter 20

Lily had discovered Hideaway Café by accident. It operated out of a tin shed by the harbour in a tiny settlement of less than one hundred people, located at the end of a gravel road that wound its way through the banksia and wildflower plains of coastal vegetation to the sea. A small fleet of trawlers berthed there, and the café sold seafood caught that day straight from the boats with fresh salads and hot, crispy chips. There were also a couple of vegan dishes. The seating area outside under a shelter had long shared wooden tables and benches overlooking the water.

Lily and Freya ordered chickpea-and-kale fritters with a basket of chips and a salad to share. Lily produced a bottle of white wine from an esky in the boot of her car, and they took it to one end of a long table where they sat side by side so they could look out at the water. A man and woman with a small child settled next to them, their giggles and quiet chatter almost unnoticed.

Lily poured wine and shooed away a hopeful seagull that perched on the end of the table.

After the catharsis of her confession, Freya sat silently, as if polite conversation had drained away with her earlier words.

Lily glanced sideways at her. If Freya was worried she'd shared too much, said things that couldn't be recalled, then she might retreat into her brittle shell. But Freya sat with a small smile on her lips, the corners of her eyes crinkling as she watched a trawler chug out of the harbour entrance, a noisy flock of seagulls swooping in its wake.

"I've been here once before, but it was only a takeaway then. It's grown and changed."

"Like us." Lily clinked her glass against Freya's.

Freya shifted on the bench so she was angled towards Lily. "Yes. Like us." She set her glass down and rested her hand on top of Lily's free one. "Thank you for persevering. It would have been easier to let me maintain the space between us."

"I guess that's not my style." Lily turned her palm up and entwined her fingers with Freya's. "If you live so close to someone, it helps if you get along."

"It helps if you like the same type of music," Freya said deadpan, "when the party wall is so thin."

"Cushion barricades work."

"Ever heard of earphones?" Freya's smile flickered. "We might have to do some negotiation around music choices."

Lily tilted her head on one side. "I seldom hear any music through the wall. Just those meditation soundtracks."

"I like Bach. Vivaldi. Judy Garland." Freya swirled the wine around in her glass, and the glance she shot Lily was pure mischief. "And AC/DC and the Sex Pistols."

"I haven't heard any punk coming through the wall."

"Dorcas hates it. She screeches louder than Johnny Rotten if I play it. I love my cat, so my headbanging days are over."

"Poor Dorcas. Does she sleep on your bed?"

"Of course. I'm not quite the crazy lesbian cat lady, but I like the feel of her snuggling in."

Lily leant in so her mouth was close to Freya's ear. "I like the feel of you snuggling in too."

"Why are you whispering?"

Lily inclined her head to her other side. "I don't want to put ideas into little heads." A wide-eyed pre-schooler stared up at them, chips crushed in his hand.

The child leant against Lily. "My mummy and daddy snuggle in bed too," he informed them. "I'm not allowed in with them when they are having special cuddles."

Lily's mouth twitched. "That's probably a good idea, sweetie. Special cuddles are for big people." She glanced across at the child's mother.

The mother grinned. "Sorry. I swear Eli's ears are the longest in Queensland. The lady's right, Eli," she said. "Special cuddles are for mummies and daddies." She smiled at Lily and Freya. "Or for mummies and mummies."

Eli carefully put his squashed chips down on the table. "Are you mummies?"

Freya's shoulders shook with amusement. "No, we're not."

"If you have special cuddles you will be," Eli informed them solemnly. "That's how my mummy got me. Why don't you go home and practice, so that you can have a little boy like me?"

His mother rolled her eyes. "Eli, we are going to have a conversation very soon about what you say to strangers."

Eli's father leant past his wife. "Sorry. I hope he hasn't embarrassed you."

"Not at all. It's rather cute actually." Lily waggled her fingers at Eli.

"Not so cute when he's banging on the bedroom door asking for ice cream when we're trying to have a special cuddle." The mother stood. "On that note, we'll leave you to your evening. Enjoy yourselves."

The family gathered up their things and a reluctant Eli and departed.

"Special cuddles. Maybe I can use that as a marketing trick." Lily sipped her wine, and her eyes sparkled wickedly over the rim of the glass.

"Maybe I can dream up a yoga pose with that name."

"Maybe we can try it out alone first."

She had always thought Freya's eyes were the piercing silver of a blade, but now in the subdued lighting and gentle mood, they were the muted softness of beaten pewter. Lily couldn't move; her limbs were heavy, transfixed in the warm gaze of the woman next to her. Desire coiled sweetly in her belly, and her breath hitched in her throat. "Freya, later, this evening—"

"Number forty-seven? Vegan fritters?" The server stood there with a full tray in his hands. "I've been calling your number for ages. Thought I'd bring it over."

At Freya's nod, he set the tray down.

"Thanks." Freya turned a brilliant smile on him.

Lily went to get cutlery and napkins, and when she returned she sat opposite.

"Don't you want to look at the view?" Freya pushed her plate and glass over to her.

"The view's better this way." The hokey line was worth it to see Freya blush.

"Thank you."

"I thought you were intriguing the first time I met you. I've always fallen for people who interest me, rather than simply attract me."

"Like Inga?" Freya's words were hesitant, as if Inga's name might spoil the mood of the evening.

"Yes. Like Inga." Lily picked up her knife and fork. "You can mention her name. It doesn't hurt anymore. I've reached the fond-memories stage of a breakup, and she's still my friend." She nodded at the bottle of wine on the table between them. "This is another of her wines."

"You're obviously better than me at moving on." Freya's words were wistful and her gaze followed the path of a small boat out on the calm water.

"Hey." Lily put down the fork and touched the back of Freya's hand. "There's never been any predetermined period for grief and healing. And because I loved Inga, I now truly feel glad she's found happiness. Of course, that conclusion took a while to arrive at. There were plenty of tears and angry words and grief. It was different for you, though, with Sarah. Different situation." She took a deep breath. "But now, I have a difficult question for you."

"Will I like it?"

"Depends." Lily held up a small bottle. "Do you put chipotle sauce on your fritters? Think carefully. This could be a deal breaker in our potential relationship."

"Only if you take the last of it and there's not another bottle. Now, share that sauce, or it will be war."

Lily poured a generous amount over her fritters. She shunted the bottle to Freya and reached for a handful of chips. "Heaven. Hot chips and spicy sauce."

The fritters were tasty, the chips deliciously satisfying, and the salad fresh.

Lily's fingers collided with Freya's as they both reached for the last chip. She snagged it away and held it up triumphantly. "Mine!"

"If you must." Freya's grin was rueful. "I've eaten enough. More than I usually eat in an entire day."

Lily ate half the chip and handed the remainder to Freya. "It's allowed. Especially when it's good food like this."

Freya wiped the chip in the remainder of the hot sauce. "I don't buy chips often. Too greasy. These are good, though, nice and dry." She ate the potato. "Dorcas eats chips. She sits on my lap and nudges one off the plate with a paw. Then she crouches on the table and stares at it until it's cool enough to eat."

"I'm horrified!"

"About what?"

"I'm not sure which is worse: that you let her on the table or that you let her eat chips. She'll teach Mabel bad habits."

"Mabel might teach Dorcas good ones." Freya paused and her head tilted to one side. "The food is gone."

"Yes."

"The wine too."

"I know." The softness in Freya's face warmed Lily to her belly, stirring the simmering pit of desire.

"Shall we go home?"

In answer, Lily stood and held out her hand.

It was a shorter drive home along a different route that took them down a gravel road through the scrubby inland vegetation. Freya watched Lily's hands, sure on the wheel, handling the little car with an easy skill. The headlights flickered off silver-grey trunks of gum trees and the tangled understorey alongside the forest road. A wallaby watched them pass, and although Lily slowed, it stayed put.

Freya's stomach twisted. Part of her wanted this drive to be over so they could move into the next stage of their lives, but part of her wanted it never to end. She stole a glance at Lily, who was intent on the dark road. Lily must have sensed her gaze as she flicked a glance to Freya and reached over the gearbox to squeeze her knee. "We'll be home soon."

Home.

She took a breath and it settled the butterflies dancing polkas in her stomach. How long since she'd gone home with someone knowing how the evening would end up? Anticipating the touch of skin on skin, of hot, wet kisses, of fingers and tongues on each other's bodies? Three years since Sarah died. Ten years since she'd made love with anyone new. But even as the doubts twisted in her head, she drew a calming breath, banished them for the pleasure of the moment.

This was what she wanted. This was her chance. Moving on. She closed her eyes and in the darkness of her head, the light of passion flared, coiling its way down to between her legs. The hollow ache of need settled low in her belly. Her breath shuddered.

Would this drive never end?

It was twenty minutes before Lily parked in front of their shops. In the shared entranceway, Lily pulled Freya closer. Her arms clasped around Freya's waist, and her breath stirred her hair. When Lily bent her head to claim Freya's lips, Freya opened underneath that soft touch like a flower. Her nipples ached with the need to be touched. When Lily's tongue traced Freya's lower lip, the touch sent a path of white heat to her nipples. And lower.

Lily drew back. "What shall we do? We can say goodnight now, if that's what you want."

"No." It was a heavy, drawn-out word. "That's not what I want."

"Do you want to come up?"

Freya was silent. Lily's place, Lily's bed, the big wide bed where she had already slept. Another time. But now, for this cycle in her life to close, that wasn't what she needed. "My place."

"Are you sure?"

Considerate Lily. She must know the enormity of that choice.

"Yes, very sure. I need to make this our time." She unlocked the door and led the way through the darkened shop, stepping unerringly around the displays, Lily's soft footfalls behind her.

Her flat was in darkness. The balcony door was part open and the soft night sounds were muted. Dorcas met them in the living area, winding her body sinuously around their legs. A soft mew, and a second smaller furry shape appeared.

Lily picked up Mabel and the little cat butted her under the chin. "I left the balcony door ajar for her too. She must have found her way across." She set the cat down and Mabel scampered over to Dorcas, and the two of them jumped up on the table where they sat and regarded their owners unblinkingly.

"Dorcas has taught her bad habits already."

Now that Lily was here, Freya didn't know where to begin. She moved to the kitchen. "Water?"

"Please." Lily watched her with slumberous eyes as Freya filled two glasses.

"Some more wine?"

"No thanks."

"Something to eat?"

"After all those chips? Freya, all I want is right here in front of me."

Her pulse jumped like a wallaby caught in the headlights. She couldn't do this; it was too sudden, too soon. But then Lily caught her hand and raised it, pressing it to her breasts. Her fingers caught the judder of Lily's heartbeat.

"It will be okay." Lily's words fell softly between them. "And if it's not, we'll stop. It's as simple as that."

"It will be more than okay. This is our time. It starts here."

"Here." Lily echoed and her fingers tightened over Freya's, holding them to the soft, dark skin of her chest.

Her calmness seeped into Freya's bones and with it came the reassurance. This was the right thing to do. She lifted her fingers from Lily's breast, and turning her hand over, pressed a kiss to the palm. In silence, she led Lily to her bedroom.

The room faced west, and the evening star still hung in the sky, visible through the window. A eucalypt brushed the glass with silvered moonlit leaves, the dry foliage scratching the pane. Freya's bed was only a double, and her sheets were an austere white. She tried to see the room through Lily's eyes and ran her glance over the white sheets, the thin doona folded to the foot, and the two pillows side by side. The room was adorned only by a single nightstand with a couple of books and a water bottle resting on the surface. Her clothes hung on an open rail, with woven straw bags underneath for the small items.

"I like to have the windows open to the sky." Freya gestured to the bare frames. "The light doesn't keep me awake. I hope that's okay for you."

"Yes." Lily moved further in and turned a slow circle. "This is exactly the sort of room I would expect you to have. A serene space. Uncluttered. I like it."

A soft meow announced Dorcas's arrival. Freya scooped her up and set her outside the door and closed it in her face. "Not tonight, kitty cat."

Freya turned, and the desire that flared in Lily's eyes warmed her. Her fingers moved to the buttons of her top and she flicked them open. When the top hung loose, she moved to shrug it away, but Lily closed the space between them. She took Freya's hands and spread them wide so her shirt gaped open. baring her braless breasts to the half-light.

Lily laid her palm on Freya's chest, covering one small breast. The taut, rosy nipple peeked through her spread fingers. Little shocks jumped down Freya's body at the contact. Lily bent and touched her tongue to the peak. Freya's knees trembled and she wound her fingers into the thick silk of Lily's hair.

Frantic thoughts tumbled and tangled in her brain. The pleasure of the here and now warred with the memories seeping into her head of the last time she had made love in this room. But then Lily moved her hand away and closed her lips over Freya's nipple, flicking the tip with her tongue whilst her fingers meandered their way over to the other breast.

Freya's eyes shuttered and Sarah's face flickered briefly behind her closed lids. But in the shifting colours of pleasure, as Lily's mouth mapped a leisurely path to the other breast, Sarah's face dissipated into the moment that was now. Freya gave a long shuddering sigh of acceptance, and her fingers tightened in Lily's hair, pulling her back up so she could kiss her.

The kiss was long and soft, and melted her bones to wax. She was pulled in to Lily's orbit, flying too close to the sun of passion.

It was right where she wanted to be.

When Lily finally pushed Freya's shirt from her shoulders so it fell to the floor, Freya worked her hands under Lily's loose top, touching the soft skin of her belly above the maxi skirt. With frantic hands, she pulled the top up and away and dropped it to the floor, leaving Lily clad in a scarlet bra of lace and satin with impossibly thin straps. The garment seemed like it couldn't possibly support her full breasts. Lily reached behind and unclipped the bra and cast it away. Freya rested her hands on Lily's shoulders, traced a pattern down her outer arm and back up the inside until her fingers circled her breast.

Around and around the nipple, until the dark centre peaked in her fingers.

The bed was only a step away, but it was too far. Freya took the pace. She paused, then lifted Lily's fingers and put them on the clasp of her trousers, then placed her own on the fastening of Lily's skirt. Taking their time, each of them stripped the other, barely touching one another's skin, fingertips brushing lightly across hips and buttocks as their remaining clothing slipped to the floor.

Freya knelt on the bed and held out a hand to Lily. One light tug and the two of them were together on the bed, the sheet kicked down to hang off the bottom. Lily's skin glowed warm copper against the crisp white sheets. Freya rested her hand on Lily's stomach, where her hips flared out from a small waist. Freya's fingers curved around Lily's hip bone. The dark patch between her thighs beckoned and enticed, drawing Freya's gaze and her fingers. She moved her hand down to cup Lily's mound, curving her fingers in to settle between her damp folds,

"Wait." Lily raised up on one elbow. In the dim light, her body was a bronze sweep. "Not without you. Never without you."

And then she moved, rolling to face Freya, her hand curving over Freya's hip to delve into the cleft between her thighs.

It had been three years since Freya had done this. Three long years, and in that time she had subdued and repressed her desires. No more. The white heat in her head built to an obliterating crescendo. Briefly it registered that the woman touching her so intimately was someone new, was not Sarah, but when the touch was so light, so skilful and seemed to know exactly how she liked it, what she'd expected to be a maelstrom of emotions and tears became a tide of pleasure and letting go.

Lily's gaze remained fixed on Freya's face, charting her reactions. When Freya's eyes widened at an unexpected pressure, Lily eased back, resuming with a lighter touch as Freya relaxed once more into the moment.

"I'd like to go down on you." Lily's voice was rough, husky with desire. "I want to know what you taste like."

The rawness of her voice, the picture the words painted, brought Freya closer to the edge. Her thighs, which had been tense with need, relaxed. Lily turned her hand so her fingers could stroke Freya's pussy lips, tickling lightly over the outer surface before slipping back to stroke her clit.

"Do you want me inside you?"

Did she? Such an intimate thing to be inside someone, one finger, maybe more, pushing in, feeling the hot, wet clasp. And herself, feeling the slip of fingers, in and out, a slow movement, a hot, wet glide. Did she?

But then Lily's finger traced a tiny circle around her clit and she was lost. The time for debate had passed. Her hips raised up off the bed in silent encouragement. The push of a finger parted her sex and slid inside. Freya bit her lip. Her mind focused between her legs, on the points of contact, on the delicious press and release of Lily's fingers. Lily wasn't forceful; she simply let her finger lie inside, her thumb passing over Freya's lips in almost idle afterthought.

Freya grabbed the sheet, clenching it in her fist. The ache of need had built to an unbearable level, and whilst she appreciated the thoughtfulness behind this slow, slow burn, it was time for more.

"Please," she whispered, her voice a husky croak, so thick was her throat. "More."

Lily's finger moved with agonising slowness, a slip and slide, her thumb a soft friction on Freya's most intimate part.

How could she survive this much pleasure? She squeezed her eyes shut tight, as much against the tears that threatened as the concentration.

"Look at me." Lily's voice was a deeper pitch, as though she, too, was battling the emotion of the moment. "Please."

The rawness of the final word made Freya's eyes fly open. Lily's face was a study of insecurity. A myriad of expressions flitted across it. "Who are you thinking of?" Lily's voice trembled, even as her thumb moved a tiny circle once more. "If it's not me, that's okay. But I'd rather know."

The tremor in Lily's voice ripped through Freya, shattering the final barrier, pushing aside the tiniest lingering doubt. This strong and beautiful woman, brought down by something as small as shuttered eyes.

"You," Freya said. "I'm only thinking of you." She looked over at Lily, at the dear face that was already so beloved. She groped for Lily's free hand, half blinded by the mist of tears. Finding it, she clasped it tight, then coherent thought blasted from her head in a suffusion of joy as Lily's finger and thumb took her over the edge and into the rosy glow of light and love.

Lily left her hand in place as the aftershocks of climax rippled through Freya's body.

Then the tears fell. Not just in a silent trickle, but in a wave of release, a flood of letting go and moving on. Lily moved to lie beside her and gathered Freya into her arms, bringing her head onto her soft breast, stroking her hair away from her damp face.

"It's okay," she whispered against Freya's hair. "It's allowed. Let it all out."

The comfort of the warm embrace was a balm long missing. Freya's tears sprung from a place she hadn't know she still kept, a wellspring of emotion pent up by the wall of self-control. Every gulping sob, every heaving breath, every dampness on Lily's skin was a release. Gradually, her tears eased enough to regain control. Her breathing pattern helped, calmed and soothed. And Lily's hand, stroking her skin as if Freya were a skittish filly. Freya lifted her head. The dampness on Lily's cheeks surprised her. Freya raised up on one elbow and bent to kiss her lover.

Lover. A word she had pushed out of her vocabulary, one that should never have applied to her again, but one that now sat comfortably in her mind. *Lover.*

"Thank you," she said. "For more than you know." Her fingers clenched with the desire to touch Lily, to learn her body, to complete their joining.

Her fingers rested on Lily's collarbone, and she traced its jutting shape. The full breast was just below, a pillowy softness, inviting to touch and taste. Her finger strayed closer, towards the dusky nipple.

"No." Lily raised up, and Freya's finger fell away. "Not now. Next time. This time is for you, only for you." She leant forwards and touched her lips to Freya's forehead.

Freya swallowed. The gifts kept coming, both in words and actions. "No," she said, even as the urge to fall back on the firmness of her mattress and rest her head on Lily's breast again and let their breath synchronise overwhelmed her. "I can't let you—"

Lily pressed a finger to Freya's lips. "Sssh. We will have our time again. There will be time and enough and more. Maybe even tomorrow. What you let me do meant a lot to me. I want to savour that."

The simple words warmed her. She turned to press a kiss to Lily's shoulder, her body already relaxing into the soft bonelessness of sleep.

"Thank you." One swift indrawn breath, a long exhale and the patterns behind her eyes were the shifting colours of dreams, shot through with images of Lily.

Chapter 21

LILY DIDN'T KNOW WHERE SHE was for a moment. The light slanted through the window in a muted, diffuse way and the room was cooler than her bedroom. She raised on one elbow, seeing the grey-green leaves of the tree outside the window.

In the small bed, the woman beside her slept on. Her silver-streaked hair was spread over the pillow, its wiry halo subdued. *Freya.* Lily studied her lover as she slept. Freya's face was relaxed, her shimmering defensive shield absent. She lay curled on her side facing the window. The sheet rested just below her shoulders, hiding her small breasts from Lily's gaze. Beautiful breasts, smooth and creamy, a dusting of freckles on the upper curve, and rosy nipples that hardened in an instant.

A light scratching noise sounded at the base of the bedroom door, along with a plaintive meow. It was the scratching that had woken her. She got quietly out of bed and opened the door. Dorcas and Mabel tumbled in and leapt onto the bed. Dorcas nestled in the small of Freya's back and glared at Lily. Mabel kept going off the other side of the bed and stalked the room, tail quivering as she explored.

Lily's glance flitted between the woman and the bed that she had just left, and the doorway to the kitchen where there would be coffee.

Freya muttered in her sleep and rolled onto her back, just missing Dorcas, who moved to crouch like a small rounded hillock on the pillow.

The bed was a lot smaller with Freya sprawled in the middle of it, so Lily headed for the kitchen. Freya didn't have a coffee machine, but Lily found a plunger and a packet of ground coffee. By the time she returned to the bedroom, full plunger and two mugs in hand, Freya was stirring. Lily put the coffee down and sat on the edge of the bed.

"I thought I'd dreamt last night." Freya pushed the disordered mess of hair from her face.

"As long as it wasn't a nightmare."

"Definitely not. It was rather erotic actually."

Lily pushed down the plunger. "Coffee?"

Freya's glance flicked from the plunger to where Lily, still naked, sat on the edge of the bed. She rolled onto her side and propped her head on a hand. "I was thinking of something a little different to coffee."

It was suddenly hard to draw a breath. The room was too warm, and she was thirsty—both a physical thirst and for something else entirely. The first she could do something about; the second… Right now, that was up to Freya. She poured a mug of coffee and took a sip. Strong and black, it burned her mouth.

"Impatient." Amusement resonated in Freya's voice. "What else can't you wait for?" She traced a line along the outer curve of Lily's thigh with a finger.

Lily didn't even pretend to misunderstand. "I can wait. I'd rather you were sure. No morning-after regrets, no second thoughts."

"None." The fingers crept higher, stroking over Lily's hip, tickling the sweep of her hip bone. "My only regret is that I didn't do this to you last night." The fingers moved up, mapped a path to Lily's breasts and lingered on the underside of one, stroking the curve.

"I don't regret it." Lily captured the wandering fingers and clasped them to her chest, stilling the movement. "Last night was for you."

Freya's fingers fluttered like a captive bird in the cage of Lily's hands. Freya tugged her hand free and levered herself upright in the bed. She cupped Lily's cheek. "And this morning is for you."

How had she ever thought Freya's eyes were cold? There was no cold mercury glare this morning; the grey eyes were the softness of unfurling petals.

Freya leant forwards until her lips hovered over Lily's. "I want this. Do you?"

The yearning in the words made Lily swallow hard. She had desired this for a long time. Had thought it was a place she would never be. This morning still had the unreal air of a dream, something nebulous she had to knot her hands into, to grasp before it could fade away. But then Freya's fingers slipped from Lily's cheek, down over the sweep of neck and shoulder to cup her breast in the same deliberate, careful way she had cupped her cheek. But her fingers danced over Lily's nipple and the shocks of pleasure sent spirals of desire deep into her belly. Freya's fingers mapped a careful path to Lily's other nipple. Lily closed her eyes, the better to focus on the ache building low and hot. An image of Freya burned behind her closed eyelids. She opened them again, wanting to see the real woman who was causing such joy.

"Stand up." Freya issued the command in a husky voice, as if she couldn't speak with a clear throat.

Lily stood, helpless in the face of Freya's authority.

Freya's hands came to rest on Lily's hips, her fingers spread.

Lily's knees trembled. Surely Freya must smell her arousal. She could smell her own musky heat, all hot and yearning. For long moments, Freya studied her, her glance flickering over Lily's belly, her womanly hips, and lingering on the junction of her thighs.

The clasp on her hips shifted, lower, more central, so that Freya's fingers pressed on Lily's belly, and her thumbs moved lightly over her pussy lips. Just a gentle touch, just a slow, tortuous to and fro, tickling over their engorged fullness. Freya bent forwards and kissed Lily's belly, her breath hot on Lily's navel.

Lily wound her hands into Freya's hair. Despite the humidity and heat of a Queensland summer, it still sprung from her head in a crinkly mass, gold and silver blending to some fantastic new colour. Lily shifted her stance so there was a gap between her legs. Freya took full advantage and her fingers trailed lower, touched briefly on Lily's upper thighs, fingering lightly before reversing to inch up the inside curve. Her finger touched Lily's lips.

Lily's fingers tightened in the wild hair. The buzz in her head was anticipation, and a joyful bubbling release. What would Freya do next? She must surely feel her damp desire, must surely realise how much Lily wanted this. *Wanted her.* Her knees shook again, a fine tremor, but she was caught in the web of Freya's weaving and she couldn't—didn't want to—move.

Freya's lips moved down, over the curve of Lily's belly, and her fingers moved up, briefly dipping between her lower lips.

A swirl, a light fingering, then the fingers crept up even as her mouth moved down and the two met and melded right above Lily's mound. She looked down at the silver-gold head and the fingers and mouth working such magic on her belly. What would that mouth feel like if it moved lower? Was that something Freya liked to do?

And then she *was* doing it, and Lily shifted position to allow Freya's lips and fingers to come together at the junction of her thighs. The lightest of touches and then the movement of her lips combined to create an explosive symphony that threatened to overwhelm her in its intensity. Her breath came in hard, hot pants, bursts of sound that rose in intensity.

Freya lifted her mouth long enough to say, "Put one foot on the bed."

Years of yoga made it easy for her to raise one leg, balance, and rest her foot on the mattress. Warm air caressed her sex, and then Freya's lips were there once more, mobile lips, agile tongue, and despite the yoga training, despite her strong thigh muscles, she would have crashed to the ground as her knee shook if it weren't for the anchoring clasp on her lover. She moaned with the joy of it, a high keening wail that grew louder with each tiny peak.

When the wave of pleasure passed, she sank to the bed, bringing her feet up to lie in the middle. Gripping Freya's hand, she urged her alongside. Freya's slighter body burned hot and she moved over half on top of Lily. Her firm thigh rested on Lily's softer ones, and Freya's nipples pressed hard points of urgency into Lily's side.

Lily kissed her, content to let the slow burn reach a simmer, and then a boil. Soft kisses, ones that tasted and sipped rather than demanded. "You're incredible," she whispered into Freya's mouth, and her hands glided a long slow journey down between her lover's thighs once more, as Lily delighted in how this pathway already seemed familiar, as if they had been joined for a long time, instead of simply the night.

Maybe for a long time to come.

But right now, the time was for pleasure. For touching and being touched and the soft, hot feelings of lovemaking.

They moved from the bed only when the morning became too hot, the movement of air from the ceiling fan insufficient to cool them. Neither dressed properly. Freya pulled a loose cheesecloth dress from the rail, and Lily found a sarong that she wrapped around herself. Freya made strong coffee, throwing away the pot Lily had made that had gone cold in the heat of their loving. The balcony was still partly shaded, so they sat on the lounger there, sipping coffee. Loving had worn away Freya's sharp edges, and the silence that wrapped around them was a comfortable one.

Dorcas and Mabel appeared from some secret hidey-hole and jumped onto the arm of the couch, purring.

Lily rubbed the head of her little cat, smiling as Mabel arched against her hand. "These two are getting along well."

"They are."

Was it too early to suggest removing the lattice dividing their balconies? It would make things easier for the cats, but it implied an intimacy that was a step above the night they had shared.

"I hope we can do this." Freya's quiet words echoed the questions in her own head. "This seems so right at the moment, but I hope we can keep it that way. We live so close, share a building."

Lily's breath huffed over her cooling coffee. "We don't have to rush headlong into anything. We have our separate spaces."

Freya gave a jerky nod. "Yes. I haven't had to share my day-to-day living for a long time now. It might be a little overwhelming at first. I hope you can understand."

"There's no timetable we have to follow."

"This, though." Freya indicated the balconies with a wave of her hand. "Maybe we could take down the lattice? Make it a shared space?"

"Did you just crawl into my head and steal my thoughts?" Lily put her coffee down on the table. "This is the perfect place for us to see what we can be together."

Freya stared down the street, her gaze following the path of a solitary pedestrian. "I hope we can be many things to each other. In time." She sat up abruptly. "But right now, we better find some clothes and prepare to negotiate our first meeting with a friend as a couple."

"How can you know that?"

She indicated the pedestrian with a nod. "That's Carly. I suspect she's coming to see if you or I fancy breakfast."

Lily glanced down at the curve of her breasts revealed by the slipping sarong. "She'll know something has changed. Does that bother you?"

"No. I'm not hiding." Freya stared into her mug for a moment as if scrying the future. "This is something I never expected to have in my life again. And I know it's the opposite of what I've been teaching—that women don't *need* to have someone in their lives to be happy. I've tried to show that independence is a good thing. But I'm not going to deny what we have." She touched Lily's hand. "So, in about two minutes, when Carly arrives, she's going to be very surprised."

"I should shower before breakfast." Lily set down her cup. "I wish I could walk along the balcony railing like the cats do. It would be so much quicker."

The bell rang and Freya got to her feet. "No time. Prepare for the onslaught!"

Lily stayed where she was, hearing Carly's chatter as she bounded up the stairs. Life for Carly seemed to be on the up.

"…and it was really good being in my flat last night. It's a nice place. I curled up on the couch—the one Remy helped me choose—and got a takeaway pizza. With anchovies, just as I like. Andy would never let me order them; he said they were disgusting things and made my breath stink. I had a glass of red wine—"

"Just one?" Freya's teasing tone drifted out to where Lily sat.

"It was a large one. And I watched a rom-com." A sigh. "I'll be okay, Frey. I will. I came to see if you and Lily wanted to come for break— Oh!" She stepped onto the balcony. "You're here early!" She kissed Lily on the cheek. "I came to see if the two of you want to go for breakfast."

"Sure." Lily looked at Freya. "I'm up for it."

"Me too. But you'll have to wait whilst I shower. Ever heard of the telephone, Carly?"

"I texted both of you. Last night and this morning. Guess you didn't look."

"Must have been busy," Freya said with a poker face.

Lily stood and hitched the sarong up so she was decent. "I need a shower too. Suppose I meet you both here in twenty minutes?"

"Sure." Carly cocked her head to one side. "Freya has a sarong just like that. Did you buy it in her shop?"

How was she supposed to answer that? She snuck a sideways glance at Freya, but her head was bent as she stroked Dorcas. "I'll be back soon," she said, and fled before Carly could put two and two together.

By the time she returned, Freya, too, had showered and dressed. Her denim shorts were faded from many washings and softly clung to her lean hips. The loose cotton top left her arms bare. Lily's gaze caressed her upper arms, and the slant of collarbones revealed by the top. The freckles she'd kissed so recently that dotted the skin of Freya's chest were only partly visible. Lily swallowed, remembering the trail of those freckles and the delights they led to. Should she kiss her in greeting? Would Freya want that? She didn't know. The nuances of their fledging relationship were still to be learnt.

Freya grabbed the cotton bag she used to carry her purse and keys and slung it over her shoulder.

My lover. The words still seemed new and fresh. Lily fiddled with the strap of her own bag.

Then Freya turned to her. "Ready?"

She nodded, the words deserting her in the softness of Freya's gaze. "Where's Carly?"

"Loo." There was the sound of the toilet flushing. "Carly will be out in a minute." Freya stepped closer. Her eyes were huge and luminous. Soft, as if her thoughts were the echo of Lily's.

"She will." The urge to kiss the parted lips in front of her was strong, but mindful of Carly, she contented herself with a squeeze of Freya's fingers.

Freya squeezed back, and turned towards Carly. Their linked fingers swung between them.

"You still want to go to the Green House, Carly?" Freya's voice had the same crispness as usual. "Now that you work there, would you rather go to Oncey-One's?"

"No way. Remy does the best breakfast. And I like to give her the business."

"Job security, right?" Lily fought the urge to look down at their joined hands. Freya's thumb passed in a quick one-two caress.

"Yeah." Carly paused and seemed for the first time to see just how close they were standing. "You two seem to be getting on well." Her gaze fixed on their linked hands.

"Did you expect us to be at each other's throats?" Lily asked.

"No. Not anymore. But this is different. Is this more than just a new neighbourly accord?"

That squeeze of the fingers again. "You said you'd like to see your friends get together." There was a tease in Freya's voice.

"I did," Carly agreed. "But you both told me it wasn't going to happen." Her eyes narrowed suspiciously "Is this some kind of crazy wind-up? Get me sucked in and planning your wedding, and then you'll tell me it's all a joke?"

"No joke." Lily reached out with her free hand and touched Carly's arm. "But it's new."

"You're the only person who knows." Freya rubbed Carly's shoulder.

"Is it a secret?

"No." Conviction shone in Freya's voice. "Of course not."

"That's good." Carly gathered the two of them into a tight hug. "Because there's a whole gang of people going to the Green House for breakfast. Remy of course, us, Alicia, Faye, Miriam, and Janie. Apparently, Janie has a new woman she met on some dating site. The brekky is for her to meet Janie's friends. I'd hate for you two to have to hide." Her arms tightened. "I love you guys. You were there for me. I'm really happy for you." With a loud, wet kiss on their cheeks, Carly released them.

Lily and Freya exchanged a glance. All these people hooking up might be difficult for Carly to handle. "You're okay with this?" Lily asked.

Carly bent to pick up Mabel, who was mewing plaintively at her feet. "Why wouldn't I be? I'm glad my friends are happy." She narrowed her eyes. "As long as you don't go all lovey-dovey and exclusive on me and don't want to spend time with me anymore."

"You should know us better than that!" Lily stuck her hands on her hips. "This is day one of a relationship that will take a lot of negotiation. We *need* you, Carly."

"Good." Carly set Mabel gently back down. "Now that's settled, let's go and eat before I faint from starvation."

As Carly clumped down the stairs, Lily hung back. Once more, she entwined her fingers with Freya's. "We can do this. You and me. A steady pace, a step here, a small advance there. Open communication. Our own private spaces. Let's see how we go."

Freya leant in. Her breath was warm on Lily's skin as she said, "I think we'll be fine."

Epilogue

THE DAY THE LANDLORD GAVE them permission to add a connecting door between their living spaces, Lily entered Freya's apartment to find her standing on a trestle, small pots of paint at her feet. Her lover wore brief shorts and a paint-splattered singlet, and her wild hair was subdued by a turban.

Freya turned as she entered, and stood waiting. Tension shimmered in her frame as she waited for Lily's reaction.

"You're finishing it." Lily came closer, her gaze locked on the mural taking form in front of her. Freya's mural wasn't completely finished, but it was close. The previous unfinished sketch had been erased, and the blocky outline of where the new french door would be showed on the white paint. But around that outline, Freya had continued the rainforest theme.

Lily's gaze absorbed the artwork she knew so well, passed over the painted figures of Freya and Sarah hand in hand in the forest. But now, where there had been only pencilled jungle, the rainforest bled into a river scene. The Pioneer River, the one that ran through town. There were the flat, sandy flood plains and the sweep of the river. There was a crocodile on the bank, mouth open in a grin. And walking hand in hand along the sand were two naked women.

The two of them. Lily's brown skin and sheen of black hair, and Freya, not the younger Freya portrayed with Sarah, but as she was now, leaner with greying hair. Lily stepped closer to look at the details. Freya had painted them with their bare feet sunk into the sand, and a flight of rainbow lorikeets swooping over their heads. In one corner were Dorcas and Mabel, tumbling in play. And above where their new connecting door would be were the words *A Woman's Pleasure and A Woman's Spirit*. The letters ran close together and were entwined with tropical vegetation connecting the two names.

"It's beautiful." Lily's words were soft, hushed, and her gaze never left the wall, tracing the fanciful design.

"Do you like it?" Still gripping her brush, Freya stepped down from the trestle.

"I love it. I love what it represents. I love you."

The paintbrush fell to the drop sheet as Freya wound her arms around Lily's neck. "I love you too."

"Are you ready for this?"

Lily looked up. "I am. I'm just choosing the perfect pair of pants." She was on her hands and knees in front of her wardrobe. A pile of bright clothes surrounded her.

Freya arched an eyebrow. "All this time, I thought you simply grabbed the first pair of yoga pants you laid your hands on."

"Why did you think that?"

"Purple pants paired with an ochre T-shirt. Pink-and-gold leggings with a turquoise-and-yellow top. Green-and-silver pants with a beige T-shirt—"

"That combination's okay."

"The last one, yes. It was every other colour choice that made me wonder." Her impish smile softened the words.

Lily stood, a pair of pink pants patterned with red hearts in her hands. "You're right. I normally do just grab the first thing I see. But this is different. I want this to go well. And that means picking the perfect clothes." She held up the pants. "How about these?"

"Paired with?"

"I have a silver T-shirt somewhere. I think I'll blend nicely with you if I wear that." Her gaze raked Freya from top to toe, taking in the wild hair tied back from her face, the neat grey-and-white top and pants.

Freya advanced into the room. "I love the pants. But let me choose the top to go with them."

"Be my guest." Lily sat on the bed and watched as Freya riffled through her clothes.

Freya pulled out a tie-dye T-shirt, swirled with every colour of the rainbow. "This one."

"It really doesn't go with the pants."

"So?"

"It's garish."

"So? Haven't I seen you wear this shirt with orange leggings?"

"You have, but I'm not wearing it for this class." She rose from the bed, took the top from Freya's hands, and threw it on the bed. "I want this to be perfect. For us, but mainly for you, so that you don't regret your decision."

"I haven't regretted any decision made in the last few months. This one won't be any different. And I want you to dress like this because this is how you always dress for yoga. I used to watch you, you know, when you started attending my class. You wore these crazy clothes, but you were so serene, so sure of yourself. You took so much pleasure in the movement."

"I still do. In *all* movement." Lily raised an eyebrow suggestively.

Freya didn't chuckle. "I'm serious, Lily. I don't want to change you. I want you to be you. And that includes your choice of yoga clothes. Now unless you're going in your undies, you better get dressed or we'll be late." She walked out of the bedroom, leaving Lily to dress.

Together they went down the stairs and through A Woman's Spirit to the yoga studio. The buzz of chatter fell silent. Seven women waited expectantly. Lily mentally ticked them off. Carly, of course, in her usual position for any class—right at the front. Remy, Janie, Janie's girlfriend, Suzie. A woman Lily knew by sight from around Grasstree Flat, and two strangers.

Freya turned on the background music whilst Lily lowered the blinds and dimmed the lights so the mood of the room was quiet and intimate. Freya joined her at the front of the room.

"Sex." Lily smiled at her lover.

"And yoga." Freya linked her fingers through Lily's and together they faced the class. "They go together. Welcome, friends, to the first Yoga for Sexual Wellbeing class."

About Cheyenne Blue

Cheyenne Blue is the author of the "Girl Meets Girl" series, three standalone novels with interconnecting characters. Never-Tied Nora, Not-So-Straight Sue, and Fenced-In Felix are also available from Ylva Publishing. Her short fiction has been included in over ninety erotic anthologies since 2000, including *Best Lesbian Erotica*; *Best Women's Erotica*; *All You Can Eat: A Buffet of Lesbian Romance & Erotica*; *Sweat*; *Bossy*; and *Wild Girls, Wild Nights*. She is the editor of *Forbidden Fruit: stories of unwise lesbian desire*, a 2015 finalist for both the Lambda Literary Award and Golden Crown Literary Award, and of *First: Sensual Lesbian Stories of New Beginnings*.

Her collected lesbian short fiction is published as *Blue Woman Stories*, volumes 1-3, with more to come. Under her own name she has written travel books and articles and edited anthologies of local writing in Ireland. She has lived in the U.K., Ireland, the United States, and Switzerland, but now writes, runs, makes bread and cheese, and drinks wine by the beach in Queensland, Australia.

CONNECT WITH CHEYENNE
Blog: www.cheyenneblue.com
Facebook: www.facebook.com/CheyenneBlueAuthor
Twitter: @IamCheyenneBlue

Other Books from Ylva Publishing

www.ylva-publishing.com

Fenced-In Felix
(Girl Meets Girl Series – Book 3)

Cheyenne Blue

ISBN: 978-3-95533-706-3
Length: 308 page (87,000 words)

A tough life in outback Australia means Felix has no time for romance. When the peripatetic Josie asks Felix to board her horse, Flame, Felix is delighted as she'll now see more of Josie. But there's something suspicious about Flame, who bears an uncanny resemblance to a stolen racehorse. Felix is falling hard for Josie, but is Josie all she seems, or is she mixed up in shady dealings?

Times of Our Lives

Jane Waterton

ISBN: 978-3-95533-417-8
Length: 244 pages (60,500 words)

For the residents of OWL's Haven, Australia's first exclusively lesbian retirement community, life is about not being afraid to take chances. Together, Meg, Allie and their spirited group of friends share their lives, hopes and dreams, proving that whatever the setbacks, hearts that love are always young.

Primal Touch

Amber Jacobs

ISBN: 978-3-95533-858-9
Length: 255 pages (98,500 words)

Rumors of a rare, white tiger have lured wildlife photographer Ashley Richards deep into the Indian jungle. There, she crosses paths with a ruthless poacher and Leandra, a mysterious, feral woman, who seems at one with the fierce felines she protects. In this charged, exotic, lesbian romance, Ashley faces danger, a deadly vendetta, and the clash of two worlds, which changes everything she knows.

Where the Light Plays

C. Fonseca

ISBN: 978-3-95533-421-5
Length: 285 pages (97,000 words)

Dr. Caitlin Quinn is a sophisticated, self-assured Irish art historian visiting Australia on sabbatical. That doesn't mean she can't enjoy the local scenery—especially sun-kissed Surf Coast artist Andi Rey. Their attraction is unstoppable, but their lives are moving in opposite directions. Andi doesn't need distractions, and a woman that eschews commitment spells trouble, with a capital "T".

Party Wall
© 2017 by Cheyenne Blue

ISBN: 978-3-95533-886-2

Also available as e-book.

Published by Ylva Publishing, legal entity of Ylva Verlag, e.Kfr.

Ylva Verlag, e.Kfr.
Owner: Astrid Ohletz
Am Kirschgarten 2
65830 Kriftel
Germany

www.ylva-publishing.com

First edition: 2017

Credits
Edited by Gill McKnight and JoSelle
Proofread by Paulette Callen
Cover Design and Print Layout by Streetlight Graphics